"I know what kind of woman you are!"

It would be easy to counter Max's accusation, but it was two o'clock in the morning when she finished working on a player's sprained ankle, and she was tired. Now she was angry, too. "Oh. And just what kind of woman is that, Max?" she demanded.

"A gold digger," he told her bluntly. "You've managed to get yourself into a position where you can meet young, gullible men with money who will fall for your *obvious* attractions. I always wondered how you managed to get recommended so highly for this job."

Davina took a furious step forward. "Just who do you think you are to talk to me this way? Or is it that you want me yourself? Is that what this is all about?"

Max did want her—Davina was almost sure. And he hated her—or himself—because of it. The question was... why?

SALLY WENTWORTH began her publishing career at a Fleet Street newspaper in London, where she thrived in the hectic atmosphere. After her marriage, she and her husband moved to the rural country of Hertfordshire, where Sally had been raised. Although she worked for the publisher of a group of magazines, the day soon came when her own writing claimed her energy and time. Her romance novels are often set in fascinating foreign locales, but Sally would not trade her country home for anywhere else in the world.

Books by Sally Wentworth

These books may be available at your local bookseller.

Don't miss any of our special offers. Write to us at the following address for information on our newest releases.

Harlequin Reader Service
901 Fuhrmann Blvd., P.O. Box 1397, Buffalo, NY 14240
Canadian address: P.O. Box 603,
Fort Erie, Ont. L2A 9Z9

SALLY WENTWORTH

the kissing game

Harlequin Books

TORONTO • NEW YORK • LONDON
AMSTERDAM • PARIS • SYDNEY • HAMBURG
STOCKHOLM • ATHENS • TOKYO • MILAN

Harlequin Presents first edition October 1986
ISBN 0-373-10926-1

Original hardcover edition published in 1986
by Mills & Boon Limited

CHAPTER ONE

THE ante-room outside the boardroom of the Redford Rovers Football Club was really furnished quite pleasantly and the chair was a comfortable one in cream leather, but Davina Forbes sat nervously on the edge of her seat and was immune to the décor of the room. She hated job interviews; they always made her feel as if she had to try and sell herself, like a slave in a market made to reveal her body to push up the bidding. But that analogy made her smile inwardly and relax a little. Maybe the star footballers who played for the team were bought and sold, but she was only applying for the job of physiotherapist. Although that position, too, was a very important one, she realised, becoming nervous again. Such high prices were paid for the players that they were treated with all the tender loving care of prize racehorses, cosseted and pampered to prolong their playing life as long as possible, their hurts seen to at once and their more serious injuries treated by experts so that they would get fit again as quickly as they could.

There was a large clock on the wall, but she didn't need it to know that she had already been sitting here for twenty minutes. At the moment the members of the Board were formally interviewing Bill Buckley, her present boss, who had been the team's physio for the last eleven years but who was now giving up the job to spend more time with his family, and who had recommended her for the position. Davina wanted the job, there was no doubt about that; it meant not only a big step forward in her professional career but also a large increase in salary, but the team had not only never had a full-time resident physio before, preferring to send their injured players to Bill's clinic, they had also never employed a woman in any capacity except as a clerical or domestic worker. So she wasn't surprised that Bill's interview was a prolonged one. He was probably being asked to justify his recommendation of her, and she could imagine that the debate might well become heated. There were several quite elderly men on the Board of Directors who probably held quite entrenched views about having a female in such close contact with the team. There was hope for her, though, in the fact that recently the Board had opened its ranks to admit a younger man, Maxwell Blair, who had brought a great deal of money and influence with him.

The door to the boardroom opened, interrupting her thoughts, and Bill came out. She looked up at him quickly and he gave her a wink, but there was no opportunity to talk, because the Club Secretary came to the door with him and asked her to go in.

Davina stood up, straightened the jacket of her grey suit, took a deep breath and walked in, head held high.

She had never actually met any of the Directors before, but Bill had gone through them with her and she knew more or less what to expect; even so she found the long row of about a dozen men, all with their eyes fixed critically on her, extremely intimidating. She paused just inside the door, fighting an urge to turn and run, but then her chin came up and she looked along the row, said a calm good morning in the general direction of the Chairman and walked to the solitary chair facing the long table behind which they sat.

'Good morning, Miss Forbes. Thank you for coming to see us.' The Chairman smiled at her, which was something, but Bill had told her he had a weakness for pretty girls, so that was really nothing to go by. He began to ask routine questions about her training, the answers to which they already knew because it was all in her curriculum vitae in front of them. But it gave her time to feel more at ease, which it was probably intended to do, and she gradually relaxed a little and answered more confidently, knowing that her qualifications were of the highest standard. They went into her previous experience in some detail, and here again Davina could answer with assurance, having worked in a private hospital and for a large sports complex before coming to work at Bill's clinic nearly a year ago.

After she had answered the Chairman's questions there was a momentary pause, and Davina took the opportunity to look along the line for Maxwell Blair, who was, at thirty-three, the youngest member of the Board and the one from whom she thought she would get the most support, although Bill had warned her not to depend too much on him. 'He's a cold, withdrawn bastard,' he'd told her bluntly. 'I can never tell what he's thinking. And I don't know him well enough socially to penetrate the kind of barrier he's built round himself. But he likes football, so he can't be all bad. And I think he's probably your best bet, so keep an eye open for him.'

He was sitting almost at the end of the table, on her left, looking down at the papers in front of him, his dark brows drawn into a frown, quite clearly a tall man even though he was sitting down.

'Perhaps you could tell us, Miss Forbes, why you would like this job?' another Director asked.

Davina smiled. 'For several reasons. Firstly because I've already treated several members of your B-team at the clinic, and I've always been interested in treating sporting injuries and in finding the best ways to make them heal quickly. Also I would like the opportunity to give regular treatment and look after a person until they're completely well again, not just see them if it happens to be my turn on duty at the Clinic. And I understand that the job includes opportunities to travel, which I would like to do. And there is, of course, the increase in salary,' Davina added honestly.

'You say you've already treated some of the players,' a voice to her left broke in, and she turned to see that Maxwell Blair was speaking to her. 'How did you get on with them?'

'Very well,' Davina answered promptly. 'But their injuries weren't serious, only torn muscles and a broken collarbone, which heal quickly anyway.'

Maxwell Blair made a dismissive gesture. 'I meant how did you get on with them as people?'

'Again very well,' she answered, not understanding the point of the question.

'So well, in fact, that you decided that you'd like

to get to know the first team players. And that's really why you want the job, isn't it? So that you have an opportunity to attract one of these wealthy young men with a view to marriage?'

The attack was so sudden and came from such an unexpected quarter that for a moment Davina could only stare at Maxwell Blair speechlessly, but then her cheeks flushed and she answered shortly, 'No, it most definitely is not. The only reason I want this job is to further my career. The fact that the players happen to be highly paid is merely incidental.'

'But you've just said that the higher salary attracts you,' Maxwell Blair pointed out bitingly.

'Yes, it does. But only in so far as anyone who has talent and experience merits a rise in pay, in any profession.' Davina was beginning to feel angry now at his rudeness. 'And I certainly have no ambition to live off someone else's talents when I can quite well manage on my own,' she added roundly.

'Yes, well . . . er . . .' the Chairman interrupted. 'You say you would be willing to travel with the team, Miss Forbes? Do you have any family ties?'

Davina looked thankfully away from Maxwell Blair and tried to regain some degree of composure. 'No. My parents live in Kent and I see them two or three times a year, and I have a brother who lives abroad, but apart from that I have no close family ties.'

'And no—er—fiancé or anything?'

Davina shook her head. 'No.'

Maxwell Blair's voice again intervened. 'I think what our Chairman really wants to know is whether you're living with a boy-friend and are likely to get married or pregnant and desert the Club at short notice,' he said brusquely.

'Really, Blair!' Even the Chairman looked slightly embarrassed. Nevertheless he looked at Davina interrogatively, his eyebrows raised.

'No,' Davina said firmly into the silence. 'As I've already said, I have no ties whatsoever. And I am quite free to travel wherever you wish me to go, either in the U.K. or abroad.'

'And would you be willing to sign a two-year contract with the Club?'

Davina nodded. 'Yes, I would.'

His tone sarcastic, Maxwell Blair again interrupted. 'And could you guarantee, Miss Forbes, not to get married within those two years?'

Resenting his tone, but unable to do anything much about it, Davina answered evenly, 'No one can see into the future, Mr Blair, but if I sign a contract with this Club, then, barring any incapacitating illness, I intend to keep it.'

'And would you agree not to marry within those two years? Would you sign a clause in the contract to that effect?' he persisted.

She took a moment to consider this but then said, 'I don't see why I should. Marriage isn't going to make any difference to my abilities as a physiotherapist. And as I haven't yet met anyone I want to marry and wouldn't anyway wish to start a family straight away, I really don't feel that it would be necessary.'

Maxwell Blair gave a short, scornful laugh. 'Which gives you a clear field with the players.'

Her hazel eyes sparked with anger, and she wondered why it was that the person on the board nearest her own age was being the one to put the most obstacles in her way. If it had been one of the elderly members she could have understood it, but from someone only about ten years older than herself, she had expected at least a more enlightened viewpoint. She turned to the Chairman and said coldly, 'I believe I have already expressed my views on that point.'

'Oh, yes, quite.' He looked up and down the table. 'Has anyone any more questions they would like to put to Miss Forbes?'

'Yes, I have.' Again Maxwell Blair's harsh voice was raised, and Davina turned to look at him in unhappy certainty that she wasn't going to like what was coming. 'Miss Forbes, I hope you don't object to me asking you a personal question, but how much do you weigh?'

For a moment she was disconcerted, but then rallied and said, 'As you've already asked me several very personal questions without asking whether I minded there doesn't seem to be much point in objecting now, does there?' She had the satisfaction of seeing his mouth tighten, but then realised that her caustic answer had very likely cost her the job, even if there had ever been any hope of her getting it in the face of such determined opposition. Feeling reckless now, she went on, 'I weigh about eight stone.'

'As I thought,' he commented, his cold grey eyes going down her slim figure. 'And do you really think you have the strength to cope with players who are much heavier than you are? How could you possibly help a twelve-stone man off the field, for instance?'

'Quite easily,' Davina snapped back. 'Because I'm a trained physiotherapist and know how to distribute my weight. Also I've done some judo training and know how to pick up a man twice my size. If you like,' she offered coldly, 'I could demonstrate with you now.'

From somewhere along the line a man laughed aloud, and the Chairman was smiling as he said, 'I don't think that will be necessary. Thank you, Miss Forbes, I think that's all the questions we want to ask. Perhaps you wouldn't mind waiting outside again for a while?'

The Secretary got up to show her to the door and Davina nodded and smiled at the Board, who all smiled back at her. All except Maxwell Blair, of course; he just looked at her with cold, implacable hostility.

'I think they might be quite a time,' the Secretary confided at the door. 'I'll have a cup of coffee sent up for you.'

Davina thanked him and he went back inside, so then there was nothing to do but sit and wait and try to ignore the sometimes raised murmur of voices she could hear from the inner room. A cup of coffee was brought to her by one of the catering staff; she drank it slowly, and could have drunk two more before the Secretary at last came to get her again. It had been a nerve-racking three-quarters of an hour; Davina had never been the only candidate for a job before and began to feel that instead of just sitting here waiting for the members of the Board to make up their minds, she would rather have gone straight home and waited for them to write to her with the result instead. But she supposed that this way the agony of suspense was at least shorter, if more intense.

Walking back into the boardroom, this time she

didn't bother to sit down, but stood beside the chair, her hand on the back. They say that a prisoner can tell whether he has been found guilty or not guilty by looking at the jury when he comes back into court; if they look him in the face then he knows he is free. Davina felt very much like that now and was heartened when she saw several of the men not only look at her, but smile as well.

'Well, Miss Forbes,' the Chairman began rather pompously, 'we're very pleased to offer you the position of physiotherapist to Redford Rovers Football Club on the terms stated, except . . .' he paused, 'except for one slight amendment. We wish to add a proviso that the position will be on the basis of a three months' trial. If we find that you are unable to do the job as we would wish at the end of that period the contract with you would be terminated. Is that acceptable to you?'

Davina looked quickly along the line and was not at all surprised to see Maxwell Blair looking at her antagonistically, confirming her opinion that he had insisted on this new proviso. She would be within her rights to refuse it, of course, but Davina wasn't the type of girl to run away from a challenge. 'Very well,' she said, still looking at Maxwell Blair, 'I accept.'

His eyebrows flickered slightly and for a moment she thought she saw surprise in his grey eyes, but this quickly turned to disdain and she looked away.

'Congratulations.' The Chairman stood up to shake her hand. 'Welcome to the team.'

Several other men shook her hand and one or two of them came round the table to do so, so it was not quite so noticeable that Maxwell Blair was the only person who did not offer her his good wishes.

They promised to send her a formal offer of the position and Davina left soon after, still feeling slightly dazed. She should also have felt excited and exultant, but Maxwell Blair's antagonistic attitude had completely taken the edge off her happiness. But he was a Director, not one of the players, and it was highly unlikely that she would see much of him at all.

When she got back to the Clinic and told Bill all about it, he was inclined to be angry on her behalf.

'Blair had no right to speak to you like that. He wouldn't have spoken to me like it and got away with it,' he said forcefully.

'No, but then he's hardly likely to accuse you of setting your cap at one of the players, is he?' Davina pointed out with a grin, adding, 'I suppose he did have a valid point, even if he did have a particularly nasty way of putting it over. Why was he so against me, do you think?'

'No idea,' Bill admitted with a shrug. 'As he's never met you before it can't be anything personal, so perhaps he's just anti admitting women into what's always been a man's world up till now.'

'What does he do for a living?' Davina asked curiously.

'So far as I know he owns and directs several companies, and also deals in stocks and shares. What I call a money juggler,' remarked Bill, not without a trace of envy.

'Hm. Well, let's hope he manages to keep all his companies floating in the air and doesn't drop any. Otherwise he might have to withdraw from the Board of the Rovers. Although, come to think of it, that wouldn't be such a bad thing,' Davina added with a smile.

'Not much chance of that,' Bill answered. 'From what I heard the Board went into his background pretty thoroughly before they accepted him. He's rock-solid.'

'And rock-solid in his prejudices as well, I'm afraid. I wonder if it's just the idea of having a woman physio he objects to, or if he's against women in general. Don't you know *anything* about him?'

Bill shook his head. 'I don't even know whether Blair's married or not. There have only been a couple of social functions since he joined the Club, and he came alone to both of those. Although that could mean anything.'

'I pity any woman who's married to him,' Davina said with feeling. 'What a life!'

'Well, you're hardly likely to have to see him very often, so I shouldn't worry about it,' Bill advised. 'Just do your job to the best of your ability and you'll be all right.'

Davina smiled at her boss affectionately. 'Thanks, Bill. It was good of you to recommend me for the job. I would never have got it otherwise. And especially as it will leave you shorthanded in the Clinic.'

'But you won't be starting with the Rovers till August, which gives me plenty of time to find a replacement. As a matter of fact,' he said, rubbing his nose, 'a nephew of mine has just finished college and is looking for a job as a remedial gymnast, so maybe I'll take him on.'

So Bill had had someone else in mind for her job all along, Davina thought wryly. So much for

thinking he had done her an entirely unselfish
good turn! But the fact still remained that he *had*
done her a good turn. She was very much looking
forward to starting her job with the Rovers. It was
going to be fun meeting new people and being able
to travel to new places, instead of being stuck
inside the Clinic all the time. And working with
famous people, in however small a capacity, had a
certain glamour about it that was bound to be
exciting. The job also had added advantages
because it meant that she could stay on in the
quite large two-bedroomed flat she was at the
moment sharing with a friend, Fay Walker. But
Fay was leaving to get married in a few weeks,
which had meant Davina either advertising for
someone else to share with, or else trying to find a
smaller flat of her own. However, now that she
had landed the job with the Rovers she would get
such a large increase in salary that she felt
sufficiently wealthy to be able to keep the flat on
by herself. It had been fun sharing with Fay,
because they were old friends, but it would be nice
to be able to please herself and not have Fay's
fiancé coming round so often that it almost
seemed as if he was living there too.

The only fly in the ointment, of course, seemed
to be Maxwell Blair and his insistence on giving
her only a three months' trial. But, as Bill had
said, he couldn't have anything against her
personally, and there was very little likelihood of
her meeting him while she was working for the
Redford Rovers, so Davina quite happily pushed
him out of her mind and just looked forward to
starting her new job.

Her last few weeks at the Clinic went quickly,

with Bill and his wife, Anne, giving a small party for her on her last day, and she came close to tears of maudlin sentimentality when Bill presented her with a new watch to mark the occasion. 'Remember us every time you look at it,' he instructed her firmly.

'Good grief!' Anne exclaimed. 'What are you trying to do to the girl? Do you really think she wants to remember you every day of her life?'

'And what's wrong with that?'

His wife pulled his beard in a way that only a wife could ever hope to get away with. 'Have you looked in the mirror lately?'

The day after she left the Clinic, Davina went on holiday to Spain for two weeks, coming back with a gorgeous golden tan and her already fair hair bleached several shades lighter by the sun so that it shone like a silken halo around her head. She felt fit and rested, and on top of the world because she was young and healthy and right now everything was going for her—a splendid attitude of mind in which to start her first day with Redford Rovers.

She arrived at the Club filled with eager, excited anticipation, and was directed to the Manager's office where she met not only the Manager, but also the team's trainer, Mike Douglas. Both men looked her over a little dubiously, and Mike spoke for both of them when he said, 'We expected you to be—er—a bit older.'

He didn't say it, but it was pretty obvious that he also meant larger. Davina had found in the past that a lot of people had a preconceived idea that physiotherapists all had to be big and hefty, capable of lifting people and being able to move them around. Bill Buckley certainly had been, but she would have been very surprised if he had ever been called on to do so. 'I'm much stronger than I look,' she told them.

Mike didn't look very convinced, but he offered to show her around the Club, going first to the room that had been set aside for use as her treatment room. It was a quite large, windowless room, next door to the home team's main changing room, both of which were built under the stands which held the crowd of fans during the matches. The walls of the room were painted stark white and it contained a treatment couch, a chair, an Interferaction machine, and a cabinet which, when she unlocked it, contained little besides a pair of crutches, some stretch bandages, and the ointment used with the Interferaction.

Davina looked round the room disbelievingly. 'How on earth did you manage with so little equipment?' she exclaimed.

'We hardly used the room,' Mike explained. 'Bill always gave immediate treatment on the field and if it was bad took the player along to his Clinic for treatment, or to hospital in the case of broken limbs. He really only used this room for treatment at half-time or for an injured player to wait here until the match was over and Bill was free to look after him.'

'I see.' Davina put her hands on her hips, looked again round the room and said firmly, 'Well, I shall want quite a lot of changes and improvements done before the season starts. And the first thing is to have this place redecorated. There can be few things more certain to make a player feel even worse when he's injured than to have to lie here in such a stark and ugly room.

And then I shall want a whole lot of new equipment. Bill, of course, had everything he needed in his Clinic, but as all the treatment is going to be given here in future, I shall have to have it all installed as soon as possible.'

'Fair enough,' Mike agreed. 'I was told you'd want more equipment. Do you know where to order it from?'

Davina nodded. 'I'll deal with the suppliers that Bill uses. I think I'll phone their rep straight away and get him to come over.' She looked round again. 'There isn't a telephone in here.'

'No, Bill always used the one in the players' changing room—hm, that might be a problem. I'll see what I can do about having an extension put in here for you. In the meantime you'd better use the one in my office.'

'Thanks. Who do I see about getting the decorating done?'

'The Club Secretary, I suppose. If you tell him what you want done, he'll either get our own maintenance men to do it or call in an outside firm. I'll show you round the rest of the place and then take you along to his office.'

There was no one using the changing rooms at the moment, the team not yet having reassembled after the summer break, so Mike showed her those and the showers beyond, and then the similar facilities for visiting teams, before taking her out to show her the field itself. They walked out on to the middle of the field and Davina looked round, realising for the first time just how vast the stadium was with its row upon row of empty seats. 'How many does it hold?' she asked in awe.

'About forty thousand, but we don't always get

that many nowadays. A lot of people have been put off coming because of all the violence. They'd rather watch the game at home on TV where they're safe.'

Davina hadn't noticed it before, but now she saw that there was high mesh fencing all around the pitch to keep the spectators off the field and protect the players from any bottles and cans that might be thrown at them, and there were also crush barriers to stop the crowds stampeding and people getting hurt—a rather sick reminder of the hooligan element that ruined the game for the majority of ordinary fans, but one that was becoming all too necessary whenever football was played.

'That's where you'll sit,' Mike told her, pointing to a bench near the players' entrance which was set back below the stand and had some protection from the weather. 'I sit there as well, and so does the Manager and the reserves.'

Davina's heart began to thump a little when she looked at the bench and she thought excitedly of her first match when she would be sitting there, the responsibility for the players' welfare in her hands.

Afterwards Mike showed her the administration offices, and finished up at the Secretary's Office. Mike knocked and they went in, but found that the Secretary already had someone with him. To Davina's dismay she saw that it was Maxwell Blair.

'Sorry to interrupt,' Mike said breezily, 'but I just brought Davina along to tell you about the equipment she wants and the alterations she wants done to the treatment room.' He nodded to

Davina, 'See you around,' and left her to manage on her own.

She turned to follow him, saying, 'I'm sorry, I realise you're busy. I'll come back later.'

'No, stay.' The words came in a peremptory command from Maxwell Blair. 'Just what is all this about new equipment and alterations?'

Davina closed the door and turned to face him. He was standing this time, not sitting, and she saw that she had been right about him being tall; she was five feet seven herself, but he topped her by a good six inches or more, so that she had to look up to him all the time. Trying to ignore this disadvantage, she answered steadily, 'Mike has just taken me down to see the room I'm to use, and if it's going to be a permanent therapy room then it will need decorating and I shall need a lot more equipment.'

'What equipment, exactly?'

Would he understand if she went into detail? Davina doubted it, so instead of answering his question she said, 'I was just going to telephone to a suppliers and ask them to send a rep along to give me a quote so that I can then give whoever deals with it a detailed list.' She looked enquiringly at the Secretary as she spoke, thinking he would be the person to see about it.

But Maxwell Blair said, 'You can give the estimate to me. Better still, have him call when I'm here so that I know exactly what you're ordering.'

Davina's heart sank a little, but if he was in charge of the Club's finances, there really wasn't much she could do about it, so she merely nodded and said, 'As you wish.' Then turning to the Secretary again, she said, 'About the decorating I want done; Mike said you have your own maintenance team, but I'm not sure if they'd be able to do it.'

'What did you want done, then?' the man asked, able to get a word in for the first time.

'Well, I'd like the ceiling and two of the walls covered in pine, with lights and heat lamps let into it and . . .'

'My dear Miss Forbes,' Maxwell Blair broke in sarcastically, 'may I remind you that this is a footballers' therapy room – not a women's beauty parlour!'

Davina's cheeks flushed a little, but she said steadily, 'I'm fully aware of that, Mr Blair, and I can only assume that you haven't seen the room that I'm supposed to use.'

'On the contrary, I was shown every room in the building when I first decided to accept the position of Director; I hardly think it can have changed very much in the meantime.'

Realising that this man, for some unknown reason, was going to try and thwart her at every turn, Davina looked him squarely in the face and said challengingly, 'Are you the Financial Director, Mr Blair?'

His face, already cold, became even more withdrawn. 'Why?'

Trust a man to answer a question with a question! But she replied, 'I understood that I was to have a properly fitted out therapy room here. Is that so or not?'

Maxwell Blair's mouth thinned. 'Within reason.'

'What I require is within reason. Why don't you both come and see for yourselves?'

'Why not?'

Maxwell Blair picked up some papers from the desk and moved towards her, but the Secretary said, 'Perhaps I could look at the room some other time; I'm rather busy at the moment.'

Coward, Davina thought cynically, but she merely nodded and smiled. 'Of course.'

She set off ahead of Maxwell Blair, but unfortunately took a wrong turning and had to accept his rather mocking, 'I believe it's this way,' with as good a grace as she could manage.

They came to the therapy room and she walked in ahead of him, thinking that if anything it looked worse now than it had done the first time. 'As you see,' she said at once, 'it needs a great deal to be done to it before the season starts.'

He walked into the centre of the room and looked round, the harsh light of the fluorescent fittings sharpening the hard thin lines of his face. The thought crossed her mind that he looked as if he had been ill for a long time and hadn't completely recovered. He was thin, too, for all that he had a strong frame. 'What exactly are your ideas?' he demanded shortly.

That was the third time he had used the word 'exactly' when questioning her, yet she had hardly had time enough to formulate any ideas, let alone be exact about them, but she answered to the best of her ability, saying, 'The starkness needs to be taken out of the room. And I also need to have fitted heat and infra-red lamps. I thought they could be fitted into pine panelling on the ceiling and this wall.'

'You said two walls earlier,' he interrupted.

Trust him not to miss a thing. 'I know. I wanted this wall done as well so that it could take an exercise bar and a mirror, as well as one or two exercise machines that need to be fixed to a wall. And I shall need a filing cabinet which can go over here and . . .' She went on detailing what she wanted, the whole thing becoming clearer in her mind as she talked.

When she had finished Maxwell Blair looked at her and said, 'Do you have any idea how much all that's going to cost?'

'No,' Davina admitted honestly. 'That's why I wanted the equipment company's represenative to come in to give me an estimate as soon as possible.'

'The whole thing's ridiculous—a complete waste of money and time!'

Gritting her teeth, Davina said as calmly as she could, 'Would you mind telling me why?'

'Because in three months you'll be gone and we'll have some other physio who'll want the whole thing changed to the way he likes it.'

Davina gave an inward gasp at his rudeness. 'I see,' she said acidly. 'So you're condemning me before I've even had a chance to prove myself. Has it occurred to you that I just might be capable of doing this job? The rest of the Board of Directors certainly seemed to think so, anyway.'

He gave a shrug of his shoulders which dismissed the rest of the Board. 'They allowed themselves to be swayed by the recommendation of Bill Buckley. For some reason it suited him to have you out of his Clinic, or else you coerced him into putting you forward for this job.'

Her hazel eyes widening in surprise, Davina exclaimed, 'What on earth do you mean, coerced him?'

His hard mouth thinned and he gave a short laugh. 'What a picture of innocence—but quite unbelievable.' Then, abruptly, 'But however you managed to worm your way into the job hardly matters now, because you certainly won't be staying. For a start, you don't have the stamina it takes to keep up with the players. They have a very crowded schedule to fit into the season, not only with league and cup matches, but also the European Cup, friendly matches and exhibition games as well as a host of others. And you'll be expected to attend not only all the matches but also all the practice sessions, whatever the weather. Can you imagine what it's like,' he asked shortly, 'sitting on the bench at the side of the field in freezing cold weather in a biting wind for hours at a time? And that several times a week.'

'If the players can do it, I can,' Davina retorted.

He laughed harshly. 'I very much doubt that. The players are running around the field all the time. You'll just be sitting there, watching.'

'Like all the thousands of people in the crowd,' she put in on a note of triumph.

His left eyebrow rose and he looked at her more closely, rather as if she was a kitten who had dared to use its claws. After a moment he said, 'This is my first year with Redford Rovers, Miss Forbes, and I intend to see that it's a very successful one. I won't have anyone letting the side down, whether it's one of the players—or you. And I don't intend to let any of them get involved with you and be distracted from play by seeing you waving to them from the sidelines. Do you understand me?'

'It would be difficult not to,' Davina answered,

her colour rising. 'But I've already told the Board that . . .'

'I know what you've told the Board, but I don't believe it for a minute. In my estimation you're just a little gold-digger who thinks she's on to a very good thing here. But I'm warning you that you can put any hope of that right out of your mind. You'll get your three months' trial period and then you're out.'

'Really?' Davina's hands were balled into tight fists as she strove to keep her temper, knowing that if she lost it she might just as well walk out of the job here and now. 'But you were outvoted by the other Directors when I was given this job, weren't you? Has it occurred to you that they might approve of my work and outvote you again? You're only a new Director, Mr Blair, not the whole Board. You're not running Redford Rovers yet! Maybe we'll see what they say.'

His face darkened, giving him a cruel, demonic look. 'Are you challenging me, Miss Forbes?' he asked with soft menace.

'I rather thought it was you who was challenging me,' she flashed back, adding, 'I'm sorry if you disapprove of my appointment, but women are quite capable of being physiotherapists, whether you like it or not. They are also capable of working in a male-dominated environment on an impersonal and equal level. I haven't got wedding bells jangling in front of my eyes, Mr Blair, and I resent the implication you put on my working here. I intend to do the job to the best of my ability and prove the Board's—or should I say, the rest of the Board's—confidence in me. Now, are you or are you not the Financial Director?'

Maxwell Blair looked at her with open dislike in his face. 'No, I'm not,' he answered shortly.

'In that case it's really nothing to do with you what changes I make in the room, is it?'

'Isn't it?' he answered smoothly.

'Are you telling me that you control the purse strings anyway?'

'Possibly,' he replied maddeningly. 'You'll find out when you submit your estimates, won't you?' Walking to the door, he opened it and said, 'You'll find it's a mistake to try and fight me. You'll only be digging your own grave. Come to think of it, I don't even think you'll last out two months, let alone three.' And then he turned on his heel and strode out of the room.

CHAPTER TWO

THE fresh smell of sawdust met Davina as she pushed open the door of the therapy room a week or so later. The pine boarding had been delivered and the Club's own workmen were erecting it, but she had some misgivings over their ability to do this kind of work and watched over them anxiously to make sure that they didn't make any mistakes – mistakes which she was sure Maxwell Blair would blame on her. Some of the equipment she'd ordered had arrived and was standing in packing crates in the middle of the floor, waiting to be installed, although she hadn't been able to order as much equipment as she had wanted and thought necessary for an up-to-date therapy room.

Davina sighed, remembering how, careful to keep to her word, she had informed Maxwell Blair of the equipment suppliers' representative's visit. He had been present the whole time, questioning her need for every piece of equipment and not only drastically cutting down on what she wanted, but humiliating her in front of the rep, who, in the end, hadn't known who he was supposed to be dealing with. She had tried to assert herself and argue the case for the things she wanted, but Maxwell Blair had dismissed most of her arguments out of hand, with the result that she was left with only the very basic equipment and where she had wanted two of some things, she had been allowed only one, so what she would do if two players had identical injuries during a game, she didn't know. Davina had seriously considered going over his head to the Chairman of the Board, but the idea somehow stuck in her throat; to go asking the Chairman to take her side against their newest and most influential Director would hardly be a good start to her career with the Rovers. So she had just had to make the best of it.

At least he had agreed to the pine cladding for the walls and ceiling, and now she checked that the carpenter and electrician had done their jobs properly and put the electric sockets and fixings for the lamp and lights where she wanted them. To alter them later would not only look unsightly but would give Maxwell Blair a reason to think she was inefficient. Not that he seemed to need any excuse; where she was concerned he just wasn't a reasonable man. Davina hadn't been in the job long enough to get friendly with anyone yet, so she hadn't learnt anything more about Maxwell Blair, but as far as she could make out she was the only person he went out of his way to torment. He checked on her every move and often came to the therapy room when the men were working there. He greeted *them* affably enough, using their first names, and they spoke to him respectfully, calling him Mr Blair. Which they didn't do with her. They started off by calling her 'luv' or 'dearie', and as soon as they found out her Christian name, immediately shortened it to Davy, and that was what she had been ever since.

'How is it going?' she asked George, the carpenter, stepping over the offcuts that littered the floor.

He stood back from the piece of wood he had

been nailing into position and nodded. 'I should finish it by tonight. Then tomorrow I'll start fixing the equipment in place.'

'That's fine,' Davina said with a warm smile. 'The players will have their first training session of the season on Monday, and I want to have it all installed by then in case I need it.'

The carpenter looked at the heavy crates. 'If you ask me, the first person who's going to need some treatment will be me! I'll probably do my back in trying to move that lot around!'

He laughed at his own joke and Davina joined in, although she feverishly hoped that it wouldn't happen, but just as they were laughing together the door was pushed open and Maxwell Blair strode in. His eyebrows rose sardonically. 'I should hardly think it a good idea to keep the men from their work if you want this room finished on time,' he pointed out bitingly.

'I was merely checking on the progress,' Davina answered coldly, wishing she didn't feel the need to defend herself every time he attacked her. 'George here assures me that it will be ready to use by Monday.'

'Barring accidents,' the carpenter put in cautiously.

Maxwell Blair nodded. 'I've arranged for a spare filing cabinet and desk from the general office to be sent down to you. And whatever stationery you need you can get from there, too.'

'Thank you,' she answered with stiff civility. The filing cabinet and desk were more of the things he'd refused to let her order, but if they had spares in the office it was fair enough; she didn't want to spend the Club's money unnecessarily. It had been the way he'd said it that had offended her; as if secondhand equipment was quite good enough for her to use. It had been very hard to keep her temper then, just as it was now.

His goading was deliberate, she was sure of that, but the more he did it the more determined Davina became to be as cool as possible. The more she saw of him the more she felt that it was becoming a battle of wits between them. But she still didn't know why, and she resented not only his attitude but the fact that she was fighting in the dark.

The thin smile he gave her proved that she was right—and also that he was enjoying needling her. That fact made Davina's shoulders stiffen defiantly and she said with deceptive meekness, 'George is afraid some of the equipment might be rather heavy for him, so perhaps you could arrange for someone to help him? Or maybe you'd like to help him yourself, as you're taking such a close interest in the job? You'd know then that all the equipment had been put in the right place without having to come and check every day, wouldn't you?'

For a moment Davina thought she saw a gleam of anger in his frosty grey eyes, but he merely said, 'I thought that was what you were doing.'

'Yes, I am,' she returned, 'but it's *my* therapy room and *my* responsibility.'

His mouth hardened and he bit back with a snide, 'But what guarantee is there that you know what *you're* doing?' Davina flushed and was about to retort, but he turned to George. 'When do you want someone to help you?'

'Tomorrow morning, sir.'

'Very well, I'll see that one of the groundsmen is sent along. Will one man be enough?'

'Might need some extra help when we put that thing into place,' George volunteered, pointing to a piece of equipment that toned up muscles with a series of weights. 'Weighs a ton, that does. And Miss Forbes wants it fixed into the floor.

Davina shot him a dark look. Miss Forbes indeed! He'd never referred to her as that to anyone else. But maybe he found Maxwell Blair intimidating too. And she disliked the way he immediately turned to the other man as the recognised authority, just as if she wasn't there. 'Perhaps you wouldn't mind if I came along too—just to make sure you don't install the equipment upside down,' she said coldly.

Both men turned to look at her, George in surprise, Maxwell Blair with dislike. George, scenting trouble, said, 'I've got to go and get an—er—another hammer,' and went quickly out of the room.

Blair turned to follow him, but Davina, thinking she had nothing to lose and everything to gain, said, 'Just one moment, Mr Blair. I should like to speak to you, please.'

'Well?'

He turned a stony face towards her and Davina's courage almost failed, but she said hesitantly, 'You've made it quite obvious that you don't want me for this job, Mr Blair, but won't you please give me a chance to prove myself? If I fail, then all right, I'll have to go. But at least give me the *opportunity* to keep it. I know you think I'm unsuitable, but won't you even give me the benefit of the doubt for this three months? It may be that you're proved to be right, but can't you just—just lay off me and let me stand or fall on my own merit?' Davina paused, biting her lip, aware that she was talking in clichés and probably sounded melodramatic, but unable to find any other words to put her case. She had never had to plead like this before and the words didn't come easily. Maxwell Blair was still standing with his hand on the door knob, waiting for her to finish. His face was still cold, but she thought she saw his mouth soften slightly and his grey eyes look at her with interest. Heartened by this, she went on, 'I don't know what you've got against me. Or maybe it isn't just me; maybe it's women in general or some woman in particular, but I . . .'

She broke off suddenly as she saw his head jerk up and his mouth whiten with fury. Taking a hasty stride across the room, he caught hold of her arm, gripping so hard that it hurt. 'What have people been telling you about me?' he demanded fiercely, his voice harsh and grating. 'What have you heard?'

'W-Why, nothing,' Davina stammered, taken aback and momentarily frightened by his vehemence.

'You must have heard something. Why else would you say that?'

'Say what? I don't know what you mean. I haven't heard anything about you.' Recovering a little, she said, 'I haven't been here long enough to hear any talk—any gossip, if that's what you mean. And you're hurting my arm,' she added indignantly.

He blinked, as if he wasn't even aware that he

had hold of her, and immediately let go. But he still glared down as if he didn't believe her.

'Look,' Davina began, licking lips gone suddenly dry, 'I didn't say that because of anything—well, personal. You just seem to dislike me so much and I wanted to try and put things right, that's all. I didn't mean anything by it.'

His mouth twisting into a sneer, he said, 'Is it so important to you that everyone likes you, then?' He said 'likes' as if it was some kind of dirty word.

Davina's chin came up and she answered shortly, 'Yes, it *is* important to me. Working in a tense, unfriendly atmosphere is no good to anyone, not only me but also my patients. The team are going to be relying on me to do my best for them, but no one can give of their best in a strained, antagonistic situation like this. Surely you realise that? Or maybe you do realise it,' she added coldly, 'and that's why you're creating it.'

Maxwell Blair's eyes narrowed and she thought that he was going to be really nasty to her again, but then his eyes settled on her face, seeing her defiantly flushed cheeks and the mixture of anger and uncertainty in her hazel eyes. It seemed an eternity before he said brusquely, 'You're right in that the welfare of the players should always come first—which is why I'm so against your appointment. But you don't need my help to make a complete mess of the job; I'm sure you'll manage that perfectly well on your own. Or should I say imperfectly?' he added with a thin smile that robbed the pun of any humour. 'I just hope that you don't permanently harm some valuable player in the process, either as a physiotherapist—or as a woman.' He looked at her for a moment longer, then turned and walked out of the room, leaving the door open behind him,

Davina let out her breath on a long gasping sigh, only now aware that she'd been holding it. So what did that mean? she wondered. That he was going to get off her back or not? It had been such an ambiguous reply to her question that she just couldn't tell. But she was bound to find out in time; that was all too painfully obvious. She stood staring at the open door, remembering how angry he had been with her, and trying to recall exactly what it was she'd said to provoke it. Something about not knowing what it was he'd got against women. Or one woman in particular. Yes, that was it. Her eyes widened. Had she stumbled on the reason for his antagonism? Or had he just been angry that she'd asked such a personal question? It *was* personal, she had to admit, and ordinarily she would never have asked it, but she had got pretty desperate when he had been so unforthcoming and had said the first thing that had come into her head. But there must be something in it or he would never have asked her what she'd heard about him. Which left Davina wondering just what it was she *hadn't* heard.

George poked his head cautiously round the door. 'Has he gone?'

'Yes. It's safe to come back in,' Davina said wryly.

He straightened up and walked in. 'You and Blair have a row, did you?' he asked, his eyes alight with curiosity.

Realising that she could soon become an object for gossip herself if she wasn't careful, Davina decided to squash it straight away and said firmly,

'No, not at all. He just doesn't trust my abilities to act as a foreman on this kind of thing. And maybe he's right; I've never had to design a therapy room from scratch before,' she admitted with a smile.

'You're doing all right, girl,' George told her encouragingly. 'And you want to stand up to Blair, or else he'll start ordering you about like a sergeant-major.'

Which was all very well, Davina thought, but she hadn't noticed George standing up to him. But maybe he didn't have to.

The next afternoon, the official opening of the new season, there was to be a small reception at the Club when all the players gathered together after the summer break. It was an opportunity for the players who had just been signed on to meet their new team-mates and for the local press to come along to do interviews and take photographs. Davina had been invited, and for the first time wore her new track-suit in the Club's colours and with the team's name emblazoned on the back. Some of the players' names she already knew because they were so famous, or through meeting them at Bill's clinic, but there were a lot of new faces whose names she had to try to remember. She received a few comments from the old team members on her being a great improvement on Bill Buckley and got several invitations to give a massage, but she treated all their joking remarks with smiling good humour and made a point of staying well out of the way when the photographs, both official and press ones, were being taken. But for one of the official line-up photos when the Manager and trainer were included, Mike Douglas called her over and she stood at the end of the line beside him.

Someone from the local press came up to her then and started asking her questions, but she merely told him her name, that she used to work for Bill and had taken over as physiotherapist, trying to keep it as simple as possible and refusing to be drawn when he asked her about her private life.

The first training session was on the following Monday morning, and fortunately her therapy room was ready in time. Davina stood in the middle of the room and looked round at all the new equipment. She was still far from satisfied and it was a lot less well equipped than she had originally envisaged, but at least it was a great improvement on the stark room that it had been before. It still had the shabby old treatment couch, though, because Maxwell Blair had refused to let her have a new one, and the filing cabinet, desk and chair that he had sent down from the office looked as if they had been consigned to a junk room ten years ago. The paint on them was peeling, the drawers stuck, and the chair was guaranteed to give you back-ache if you sat on it for more than twenty minutes at a stretch. Luckily there hadn't been any suitable stationery in the office for her record cards, so she had gone out and bought those herself, handing the bill over to the Club Secretary, so at least those were exactly what she wanted. But even though the room was far from ideal, she still felt a beat of excitement as she looked around her. It was her domain; she didn't have to share it with anyone or take orders any more. Although Bill had been a friend as well, he had still been the boss and she only an employee, but here she could at least feel as if she was in charge of her own actions. Except for Maxwell Blair, of course. Davina sighed, wishing the thought of him hadn't intruded to spoil her happiness.

Glancing at her watch, she saw that it was almost ten and picked up her emergency bag to go out to the pitch, her heart beating a little faster, and mentally crossing her fingers in the hope that everything would be all right.

It wasn't quite so warm today and she was glad of the lightweight sweater she had on under her track-suit. The wind seemed to pick on her bench, the vast stadium acting as a funnel that channelled the wind down to its centre. Mike Douglas was making the players work hard, getting rid of any softness that had accumulated during the summer holidays. They were doing ball work too, practising passing and control and taking it in turns to fire shots at the poor goalkeeper, who was leaping from one side of the net to the other.

Someone pulled a calf muscle slightly and Davina ran over to help him back to the bench, going down on her knees in front of him to massage his leg. He grinned down at her. 'I could stand this all day!' But he was soon back on the field with the others. They worked on until lunchtime and Davina breathed a small sigh of relief when there were no more injuries. That afternoon the players were having a lecture on tactics, so most of them stayed to have lunch at the Club, but she was free for the rest of the day. This was another reason why she liked the job; although she had to work every Saturday and a lot of evenings, as well as most mornings, she did get some afternoons off. Deciding that this afternoon she would go to the local library and then do some shopping, she went to the therapy room to put away her bag of equipment, and was about to leave when she was surprised by a knock on the door.

'Come in!' she called.

One of the players in the first team, a striker who had been with the Club for some years, came in and shut the door behind him.

'Yes? Is something the matter?'

He nodded and put a hand on his left shoulder. 'I think I've pulled a muscle in my shoulder. Wondered if you could do anything for it.'

'Yes, of course. Did you just do it today?'

'Yes, I must have knocked into someone.'

'You'd better take your shirt off and let me have a look at it,' Davina told him, spreading a piece of paper sheeting over the couch.

He did so, and sat down on the couch with his back to her.

'Is it very painful?' she asked sympathetically.

He made a 'putting up with the pain bravely' type of face. 'It is a bit, yes,' and put a hand up to tenderly touch his shoulder again. Only this time he touched his *right* shoulder.

Davina stiffened, realising he was having her on, but instead of telling him that she'd caught him out, she said, 'You poor thing. If you lie down I'll massage it for you.'

'Thanks.' He lay down, trying to keep a smug smile off his face.

'I'll just get some cream to rub in,' Davina told him, and went over to the 'medicine chest' where she kept all her creams and lotions. Picking out a jar right at the back which was a very hot muscle relaxant ointment, she first put on a pair of thin surgical gloves and then spread a large dollop of the cream on his shoulder. His grin faded a bit when he realised she wasn't using her bare hands on him, and disappeared completely when the heat of the ointment began to penetrate his skin.

'Er—that stuff's a bit strong, isn't it?'

'Oh, yes, it has to be. The heat has to get right down into your muscles before it can do them any good.' And she rubbed the cream in even harder, not being at all gentle about it.

He stood it for a few minutes more and then suddenly sat up jerking away from her. 'My God, my shoulder's on fire! What the hell is that stuff?'

Davina looked at him with wide, innocent eyes. 'What's the matter? Can't you take it?'

'Take it? Nobody but a fiend out of hell could take that!'

'Just a little longer,' she said persuasively. 'I'm sure it's doing you a world of good.'

He backed hastily away, almost falling off the couch in his hurry. 'It is—it is. It's much better already.' He moved his shoulder and gave a shuddering groan, but managed a clamped-teeth grin. 'You've done wonders. No pain at all now.'

'Really? That's good. But perhaps I'd better massage some more of this cream in just in case,' Davina offered.

But he was already picking up his shirt and backing towards the door, tears smarting in his eyes. 'No, it's okay. O-oh! It—it's fine, thanks.'

'Oh, by the way,' Davina said as he reached for the door handle, 'perhaps you could tell the next

person who comes for a massage that I have plenty
of this cream left. And it might be a good idea if
they remembered which leg or shoulder they're
supposed to have hurt.'

'Oh God!' He looked at her, realising he'd been
had, and staggered out of the room, still stripped
to the waist and heading fast for the showers.

Davina, with laughter in her face, threw the
gloves in the waste disposal and went to close the
door after him, but found Maxwell Blair standing
there, staring after the player incredulously. 'What
on earth's the matter with him?' he demanded.

'Nothing.' Davina didn't see why she should
explain and wasn't even sure that he would see the
joke if she did. And she certainly didn't want to
get the player into any trouble just because of a
silly prank.

He turned to face her, the coldness in his face
freezing her laughter away. 'You certainly don't
waste any time, do you?' he said contemptuously.

'Waste any . . . Oh!' Davina's cheeks flushed red
as she realised what he was implying. 'For
heaven's sake! I only met the man on Friday.
Today is the first time I've ever spoken to him.'

'He hardly looks as if all you've done is speak.
He looked—exhausted.'

'Well, he wasn't. And I resent . . .'

'Then just what was the matter with him? Has
he been hurt?' he asked with a note of anxiety in
his tone, obviously worried that one of the best
players might be out of the team at the very
beginning of the season.

'No. He's perfectly all right.'

'Then what was he doing here?'

Cornered by the straight question, Davina

squirmed, looking for some excuse, but couldn't think of one. 'He was just—er—here, that's all.'

'If you won't tell me I shall just have to draw my own conclusions,' Maxwell Blair pointed out icily.

'I thought you already had,' she retorted.

His jaw hardened. 'You would do well to remember, Miss Forbes, that you're here on three months' probation. I've already warned you about keeping away from the players, and that also includes not encouraging them to come to you, unless of course it's in your professional capacity. But you say this wasn't . . .?'

He left the sentence hanging in the air, waiting for her to give him an explanation, but Davina just looked up at him in stubborn silence, a pulse in her neck betraying her nervousness. His frown deepened as he said harshly, 'You realise I shall have to report this incident to the Board?'

Her chin came up at that. 'I realise that you intend to.'

'You could still give me an explanation.'

Davina looked at him for a moment, then said placatingly, 'Look, I give you my word that nothing—untoward took place. But that's all I'm prepared to say—to you.'

His eyebrows rose. 'Your word? And do you seriously expect me to believe you when a man leaves here only half-dressed and hardly able to walk?'

'It was—different from how it looked,' Davina told him rather helplessly.

'Really?' The word itself was an insult, the way he spoke it an even more cutting one. 'And what did you mean: that that was all you were prepared to say to me? Would you tell someone else what happened?'

'Possibly. It would depend on who it was.'

'So why won't you tell me?'

Davina decided that she'd had enough of this. What had started as a molehill of a joke was rapidly growing into a mountain of an incident. Picking up her handbag, she walked to the door, but Maxwell Blair put out a hand and caught her wrist.

'Wait. You haven't answered my question.'

She looked for a moment at his hand, holding her wrist in its strong grip, then raised her eyes to his face. 'I'm not going to tell you, Mr Blair, because it's quite obvious that you have absolutely no sense of humour. In fact I'm rapidly coming to the conclusion that you're little better than a sadist!' Then she jerked her wrist from his grasp and left him staring after her in astonishment.

Afterwards she cursed herself for being a fool. She should never have said that to him. She seemed to destroy any chance of having an ordinary working relationship with him every time she met him. But he got her so mad that she became nervous and always said the wrong thing. He would probably go running to the rest of the Directors now, telling them how rude she'd been to him, on top of his suspicions about her with the player. Sometimes cursing herself for an idiot, at others feeling perfectly justified, Davina walked to the local park and sat down on a bench in the sun, trying to think rationally and calmly, which wasn't easy when she felt so worked up and emotional. If only she knew why Maxwell Blair had such a down on her! But trying to work that one out was just beating her head against a brick wall. She sighed, and realised that if she wanted to

keep her job she would just have to apologise to
him. Although crawling to anyone, especially to
someone like Blair, just wasn't in her nature, and
she rebelled at the whole idea. And then he might
not even give her a chance to; he might go straight
to the Board today.

Glumly Davina got up and walked back to the
Club, knowing that she had to apologise now if it
was going to do any good. The doorman, whom
she'd got to know as 'Old Pete', was standing by
the entrance and she asked him, half hopefully, if
Mr Blair had left.

He shook his head and pointed across the car-
park to a silver-grey Rolls Royce. 'No, his car's
still here. He'll probably be in the Directors'
dining room, if you want him.'

'Thanks.' Davina walked slowly up to the room,
putting off the evil hour as long as possible, but
when she looked in he wasn't there. Puzzled, she
asked one of the clerks, who said she hadn't seen
him, and it took her a good ten minutes before she
tracked him down to the gymnasium.

He was in there alone, stripped down to shorts
and a sports vest, and he was using the punchbag.
Davina was about to speak, to let him know that
she was there, but the words died in her throat as
she watched him. He was hitting the punchbag
savagely, as if it was an object of hatred, his
gloved hands smacking repeatedly against the
leather, his mouth drawn back into a snarl as he
landed punch after punch with all his strength.
And that he was strong there was no doubt. His
arms and long legs were all whipcord muscles and
he had the slim waist and broad strong shoulders
of an athlete, a man who had always kept himself

in shape. There wasn't an ounce of fat on him, and again Davina thought he was too thin and she wondered if he had been ill. But perhaps it was just his restless, driving energy, an energy he displayed now as he beat unmercifully at the bag, driving each punch home with precise, measured ferocity. Not exercise, but a kind of emotional despair.

Davina shivered suddenly, imagining what it would be like if he had a person under his hands instead of the innocent punchbag. She turned to go, sure that this wasn't the time to interrupt him, but the door creaked as she opened it and he called out, 'Wait!' in a tone that was an undeniable order.

Reluctantly she shut the door again and turned to face him. After stripping off the gloves, Maxwell Blair pulled the sweat-band off his head and threw it aside, then brushed his hair back into place. His face was glistening with perspiration, emphasising the leanness of his features, the high cheekbones and clean-cut line of his jaw. His grey eyes settled on her broodingly, and Davina felt her heart begin to thump painfully in her chest.

'Did you want to see me?'

She nodded wordlessly, and walked slowly towards him, realising that she had never really looked at him before; seen him, of course, but not *looked* at him. Never noticed that his lashes were long or that his left eyebrow arched more than the other, or that there were faint lines around his eyes and mouth that might deepen when he smiled— only she had never seen him smile.

'Well?' he asked unhelpfully.

'I—I don't want to disturb you,' she began uncertainly.

'You're not. I'm finished here,' he answered shortly.

'Oh. Well.' She took a deep breath. 'As a matter of fact I came to apologise to you. It was rude of me to speak to you the way I did.'

His eyebrows flickered for a moment and then he stunned her by saying, 'But probably justified. I spoke to the player myself, and although he wasn't very forthcoming I gathered that he attempted some kind of a practical joke which he didn't get away with. Is that correct?'

'If he said so,' Davina agreed cautiously.

He looked at her for a moment, then picked up a towel and tossed it across his shoulders. 'Why didn't you tell me that in the first place?' he said, his voice impatient. Then, 'I suppose it was to be expected. You might even get more of the same, although I've let it be known that it isn't particularly funny. If anyone else tries it you'd better let me know.'

Shaking her head, Davina said, 'Thanks, but I can fight my own battles, Mr Blair.'

'Can you, indeed?' He looked as if he didn't believe her, but for a moment she thought she saw amusement in his eyes, and knew intuitively that he was thinking of the player she'd sent away with a burning shoulder. So maybe he *did* have a sense of humour after all. But the expression was gone so swiftly that she wasn't sure any more. 'Nevertheless I want to know if anyone else tries anything.'

He nodded dismissively and she turned to go, then hesitated and said, 'Can anyone use this gym to exercise in?'

'Anyone from the Club, you mean?' And when she nodded, 'Yes, I suppose so. Except when the players are training in here, of course.' His eyes ran over her slim figure in a plain cotton skirt and short-sleeved shirt. 'You hardly look as if you need to exercise,' he observed brusquely.

'But I like to keep fit. And I've a feeling I shall need to keep fit in this job.' She gave him a small, tentative smile.

'But hardly necessary when you're going to be here for such a short while,' he answered acidly. 'You'll be gone from here by Christmas.' And then he turned and began to pull on a track-suit, pointedly turning his back on her.

Feeling as if he'd slapped her hard in the face, Davina quickly hurried out of the room, and then ran down the echoing corridors of the stadium until she was out in the open again.

'Did you find Mr Blair?' Old Pete asked her.

'Oh, yes, I found him all right,' she answered, and wished like hell that she hadn't. For a moment she had thought that she was getting through to him, that he was halfway human after all, but that last remark had put everything back in its earlier perspective again. She had been an idiot to think it could ever be any other way. Like most men, Maxwell Blair had a one-track mind, and once it was made up nothing could change it. It was just her bad luck that the course he was set on was in getting rid of her as soon as possible.

The team's training sessions intensified as the start of the season grew closer, but there was a relaxing evening for everyone when the Club held their annual 'start of the season' dinner and dance at the local Town Hall. All the Club's employees as well as the players were invited, along with several important members of the Supporters' Club, and each invitation was for two people so that everyone could take a partner. Bill Buckley had also been invited, so Davina consulted his wife on what to wear.

'It's quite formal,' Anne told her. 'All the Directors and most of the players wear black tie, and all the official guests, of course. There are quite a few of those. It's only the very young players who are allowed to wear ordinary suits.'

'So what do the women wear?'

'Most of the Directors' wives wear long evening dresses, but most of the younger women wear short. Some even wear trousers. I remember last year there was one girl, the girl-friend of one of the new players, and she wore . . .'

Anne told her story and it was some time before Davina could get her back to the point. 'So what are you going to wear?'

'A dress I bought on holiday earlier this year. It's long but summery, if you see what I mean.'

'I hope they put me next to you two at dinner,' Davina remarked. 'Otherwise I shall be on my own.'

'Aren't you taking your boy-friend? What's his name—Peter, isn't it?'

'Mm. Peter Longman.' Davina shook her head. Peter was a schoolteacher and had gone on a tour of Greece for the summer. 'No, he's still away and won't be back until the beginning of September.'

'You don't sound very worried,' Anne observed.

Davina laughed. 'I'm not. We enjoy each other's company, but we're not serious about one another. We're just friends more than anything else.'

'What a waste! Why don't you find someone you can settle down with and marry?'

'Oh, Anne! You make it sound so easy. As if you can just walk out into the street and pick someone. Just because you were fortunate enough to meet Bill and fall for him when you were nineteen, it doesn't mean that it happens to everybody that way.'

'You don't even try,' Anne accused her. 'You've had some really nice boy-friends, but you never seem to go out with them for more than a few months.'

'Well, that's usually enough time for me to know that I don't want to spend the rest of my life with them,' Davina pointed out reasonably. 'Don't worry about me. I'm doing fine as I am.'

'I could bring someone along as your escort,' Anne offered. 'He's really nice—the brother of a great friend of mine. You'll really like him.'

'Now where have I heard those words before?' Davina stood up with a laugh. 'No, thanks. I prefer to choose my own boy-friends.'

But she did rather wish she had a partner, and contemplated phoning one of her ex-boy-friends, but although she had parted with most of them on friendly terms, Davina always made it a rule never to go out with them again once they'd broken up, and had always found it a wise policy. And she wasn't the kind of girl to go out with more than one boy-friend at a time, so, as Peter was still away, she would have to make out on her own.

The evening of the dance was fine and warm, so she had no need of a coat over her lacy black dress. Bill and Anne picked her up at the flat and they drove to the Town Hall, the car-park already quite full of cars. The Chairman of the Club and his wife were receiving the guests as they arrived and there was a small queue waiting to be announced. As Davina stood in line she was able to look into the large ante-room beyond, and almost the first person she saw was Maxwell Blair. But this was a different man from any she'd seen before. He was standing near the bar in a small group of well dressed people, talking to a very sophisticated brunette, bending his handsome head to listen to her and then smiling and nodding at what she'd said. Davina saw she had been right, the faint lines round his mouth did deepen when he smiled, making him look a different person altogether from the tyrant she knew. And his evening clothes suited him, making him look even taller and broader. And handsome too. Funny that she'd never really noticed that before.

Someone else spoke to him and he turned away, so Davina looked instead at the woman beside him, wondering if she was his wife. She exuded money. Superbly dressed, she wore a bronze-coloured evening dress that was cut very low at the back and had a large gathered frill that came up the front and across one shoulder; the other shoulder was completely bare. It looked a very exclusive dress, the kind you saw in the windows of little shops in Bond Street or Chelsea without any price tag on them. The woman herself also looked pretty exclusive; about thirty and with a good figure, her face well made up and her hair beautifully styled. Davina felt a stab of something very close to envy and wondered if the woman had ever had to work for a living.

'Miss Davina Forbes!' With a start she realised that she was being announced and hurried forward to shake the Chairman's hand.

He greeted her with pleasure, introduced her to his wife and made her promise to dance with him later on. Davina agreed mechanically, sure he didn't mean it, and followed Bill and Anne over to the bar, where they immediately joined Mike Douglas and some of the past members of the team who had travelled to Redford for the occasion. Davina was introduced to them all, someone got her a drink, and it was a little time before she had an opportunity to look round, and somehow her eyes were drawn straight back to where she had seen Maxwell Blair. He wasn't talking now, he was standing with the group but a little apart from them, and his eyes, too, were looking round the room. Their glances met and held and for a startling moment Davina felt as if they were the only people in the room. But he had no smile for her, just a curt, tight-mouthed nod, before his eyes moved quickly away again.

Dinner was announced shortly afterwards and Davina found herself seated next to an ex-player who was also on his own, on the same table as Bill and Anne, which was quite some way from the top table where the Directors sat with their wives and principal guests. There were a couple of speeches; one by the Chairman welcoming the new players, and her name was also mentioned as part of the team, which she thought was very nice of him. And one in the eye for Maxwell Blair! she thought with some satisfaction. The Chairman then greeted all the guests and a reply was made on their behalf by the Mayor, and after that the band struck up and everyone could relax and dance.

The band was a good one and soon most of the people were up on the floor. Davina danced with the ex-player two or three times and with Bill and some of the other men on their table, and as she loved dancing at any time she was thoroughly enjoying herself. Once or twice she caught a glimpse of Maxwell Blair either dancing or sitting at his table. She saw him dance with the brunette once, but that was all; whenever she saw him again he was dancing with a different woman. Probably doing his duty and dancing with every woman at his table, as most of the men were.

It was quite late in the evening when, to Davina's surprise, the Chairman kept his word and came over to ask her to dance. He wasn't a very tall man, only about the same height as her in her high heels, but he held her quite close to him in a slow smoochy number.

'And how are you settling in, my dear?' he asked. 'Perfectly happy?'

'Oh, very,' Davina assured him, remembering that he was supposed to have an eye for pretty girls and gently easing away from him.

'Good, good. Now if there's anything you want, or anything you're at all unhappy about, you must come and tell me straight away,' he told her, and pulled her close against him again.

Davina had visions of the dance turning into some kind of tug-of-war, but they hadn't gone much farther round the floor before Maxwell Blair came up to them and said, 'Excuse me, Sir Reginald, but the Mayor and his wife are leaving now and waiting to say good night to you.'

'Oh, really? Just now?' The Chairman looked disappointed. 'I'm so sorry, my dear, I was enjoying our dance.' Davina smiled and went to walk away, but he said, 'No, no, you must finish the dance. Max, as a great favour I'll let you take over from me. You and Max know each other, don't you, Davina? Yes, of course you do. Take care of her for me, my boy.' And then he gave the other man a playful punch on the shoulder and strode smilingly away.

CHAPTER THREE

FOR a startled moment Davina didn't know what to do, then, without looking at him, she started to mutter, 'It really isn't necessary. I don't . . .'

But someone almost bumped into them as they stood in the middle of the floor, and Max Blair said shortly, 'We seem to be causing an obstruction,' and put one arm firmly round her waist to draw her towards him.

Davina automatically put her left hand on his shoulder and let him take hold of her right in his cool grip, too confused to resist. And once they had started dancing it seemed impossible to break away again. She gave him a nervous glance, sure he must be hating every second and that it would show in his face, but his features were set into an expressionless mask as he looked over her head, guiding her around the floor. He didn't speak and Davina couldn't think of anything to say. Remarks like, Are you enjoying the evening? or, Isn't it a good band?, the kind of small talk you would make with a comparative stranger, seemed completely wrong somehow.

He danced well, in time to the music but no sort of clever exhibition stuff, and not so slowly that they hardly moved. If it had been with anyone else, Davina could have relaxed and enjoyed herself, but she held herself stiffly in his arms, a pulse beating nervously in her throat, wishing the music would end.

It did at last, a good five minutes later, and she again went to walk away. But it was only a pause as the musicians changed to another slow tune, and Max kept hold of her hand. She looked at him, surprised that he wasn't as eager as she was to part, and her eyes stayed on his face. This time there was emotion there; a deep, yearning hunger that showed in his tormented eyes and pinched mouth, a look that was almost of pain, unbearable pain. It was a look that Davina had never seen on anyone's face before, and it so caught at her heart that she instinctively lifted a hand to touch his face, a gesture both of sympathy and recognition.

Immediately his hand flew up to catch hers, and only then did she realise what she'd done and how angry he would be. This wasn't the kind of man who needed pity, especially from her. His fingers gripped her hand fiercely as he pulled it down and for a moment his grey eyes blazed into hers. Davina flinched, as much from the fear of his anger as from the pain of his hold, her eyes wide and scared. He glared down at her, but gradually his expression changed and his grip on her hand relaxed. His eyes grew dark, a flame of hunger in their depths—and he drew her closer to him.

Davina's breath caught in her throat; she was quite experienced enough to recognise that look in a man's eyes. But from Maxwell Blair! Him of all men?

Now as they danced on she was totally aware of him as a man, of the pressure of his hand on her waist, of his body where it touched hers and the faint, tangy-clean smell of his after shave. She felt the muscles of his shoulder move under her hand and remembered how she had seen him work out in the gym. Only then she had just seen him as a person stripped down to sports clothes, hadn't looked on him as a man at all, and certainly not as a man in whom she could ever be interested. Not that she was, of course—that was silly. Just because he'd looked at her *that* way it didn't mean she would change her opinion about *him*. Max pulled her close against him to avoid another couple and her pulse quickened. She waited for him to loosen his hold again, but he didn't, just went on dancing with their bodies together, at one with the haunting beat of the music.

Slowly Davina raised her head to look at him again. The lights in the ballroom had been turned down, there were just coloured spotlights that reflected off the mirrored ball revolving in the middle of the ceiling. They created weird effects; sometimes giving his features a look of fire, sometimes of cold green ice. But then Max turned so that his back was towards the light and she saw his face as it really was, but thinned and shadowed by the semi-darkness. The hunger was there still, she hadn't been mistaken, but much deeper now. A raw need that frightened her by its intensity and nakedness. For Max Blair made no attempt to hide it. Perhaps he couldn't, perhaps he had no power to control this sudden need that had grown out of anger.

She gave a little gasp, shocked by the primitiveness of it, and pushed herself away from him. For a moment he resisted, his hands fiercely holding her where she was, refusing to let her leave the hardness of his lean body. But then the music ended, the lights came on again and he blinked as if realising where he was. For an instant he had a stunned, incredulous look in his eyes before his face set into a closed, expressionless mask and he took a quick backward step away from her.

'I—er—I'll take you back to your table,' he said roughly, not quite in command of his voice. But he didn't touch her, merely walked along beside her and gave her a curt nod and a short, 'Thank you,' before striding quickly away.

'How did you come to dance with Maxwell Blair?' Anne exclaimed as soon as he was out of earshot. 'I didn't think he mixed with the likes of us.'

'I don't quite know,' Davina admitted, still feeling rather dazed. 'I think I was somehow coerced into it against my better judgment.'

'Why? Didn't you enjoy it?'

Davina looked across the room to where she could see Max Blair walking quickly out of the ballroom into the lobby. Of course she hadn't enjoyed it. Who could enjoy dancing with a man who probably wasn't even aware of who you were? He'd held her close, yes; but in his thoughts it was some other woman he held, Davina was sure of it. His outraged look when the music stopped had been proof enough of that. He hadn't been able to get away from her quick enough. A bitter taste rose in her mouth. How dared he *use* her like that? Davina wished now that she had refused to dance with him. But she had stayed. Because at first she'd thought that look was for her? Her thoughts melted into confusion.

'Hey!' Anne's voice brought her back to her surroundings. 'I asked you whether you enjoyed dancing with Maxwell Blair.'

'Oh, no, not at all,' Davina answered, but the

next second realised that she had enjoyed dancing with him, had liked it all too much.

The dance went on for almost another hour, but she didn't see Max Blair again and concluded that he must have left when she saw him go out of the ballroom. Too shattered by his loss of self-control to stay, she supposed. But the woman she had seen him with earlier was still here, and when Davina casually asked who she was, Bill told her she was the Chairman's sister. 'She always comes to the big social functions,' Bill went on. 'Her husband used to come with her, but they got a divorce a couple of years ago, but she still comes and usually drags some man along, though she's on her own this year.'

'Possibly on the look-out for another rich husband,' Anne said cynically. 'She looked to be making a play for Maxwell Blair earlier on, but she doesn't seem to have got very far.'

'Isn't he married, then?' asked Davina, trying to keep her voice as light as she could.

But Anne gave her a sharp glance. 'I don't know. I've never heard anyone speak of him having a wife. It would be interesting to find out, though, wouldn't it?'

Davina just shrugged and didn't answer, and she was soon dancing with Giles Allinson, one of the new players, a bachelor who was one of the up-and-coming stars of the first team. He was nice enough and obviously liked her, because he had asked her to dance several times in the course of the evening, but Davina refused his offer to take her home and wouldn't commit herself when he asked her to go out with him.

She left, as she had arrived, with Bill and Anne,

and they dropped her off at the flat, refusing her offer to come in for a nightcap because they had to get back to take their baby-sitter home.

'It *was* a good night, wasn't it?' said Anne as they parted. 'I thoroughly enjoyed it.'

'Yes, great,' Davina agreed, but as she let herself into her flat she didn't know whether she was glad that she'd gone or whether it would have been better to have stayed at home.

The football season got into full swing on the following Saturday when the Rovers played their first home match. Davina slipped unobtrusively into her place on the bench with Mike Douglas and watched as the two teams led by their captains emerged from the tunnel under the stadium on to the field, to be met by a huge roar of applause from the thousands of fans who had turned out to watch them. The Redford Rovers team wore red shirts and white shorts with red socks; their 'strip', in football jargon. The teams warmed up for a while, practising goal kicks and running around to get their muscles moving, while the fans chanted a song, waved their banners and happily waited for the game to start.

When it did the reserves came to sit with them on the bench, wondering if they were going to be lucky and get a game after all, but knowing that if they did it would be at the expense of one of their team-mates. Davina fervently hoped there wouldn't be any serious injuries; pulled muscles and strains she could cope with, but a physio could do nothing for a broken limb except sympathise for the player who knew he would be out of the game for weeks to come.

From where she sat, Davina couldn't see the Directors' box, but she knew that they were all up there, watching the game. And she was quite sure that Max was also watching to see if she made any mistakes. It was strange, ever since she'd danced with him she'd thought of him as Max, no longer was he Mr Blair in her mind. She hadn't seen him since then and hadn't wanted to. It was a meeting she couldn't even begin to envisage.

The game started with a roar of encouragement from the fans on both sides, and they never seemed to stop shouting their heads off the whole way through. Davina had never experienced such a noise; all her football watching had taken place in the quiet of a sitting-room in front of a television set up till now. It was deafening, reverberating on her eardrums in great waves of sound, and somehow she thought she'd never get used to it. But the human body is very versatile, and as she became interested in the game the noise just became a background, and she was even able to hear Mike's voice when he spoke to her.

No one was hurt during the first half, but at half-time Davina went back into the stadium with the players, ready to massage tired leg muscles back into life. One player complained of cramp, so she went into the therapy room to get him some salt tablets, then stood in the doorway in consternation. Since she had been here this morning the room, except for the equipment that was fixed to the floor or walls, had been completely rearranged. Her desk had been put over behind the door and the treatment couch moved to one side, with the movable equipment lined up neatly against the far wall. Even her medicine chest had been moved to another position. A wave of intense fury filled her and she wanted to run out and find whoever had dared, *had dared* to alter her room around. And without even bothering to tell her, let alone ask! She almost turned to go out again, but then remembered the player with cramp. He had to come first, whatever her feelings of outrage at this—this despicable interference. Snatching up the salt tablets, Davina hurried back to the players and stayed with them, following them out to the field again.

When she sat down, she immediately button-holed Mike. 'Was it you who gave orders to have my room changed round, Mike?'

He looked surprised. 'Not me, Davy. Didn't you know? It was Max Blair. I thought you knew all about it. I saw him in there this morning telling one of the maintenance men what to do. I thought you'd asked him to see to it for you or something. Although I must say I thought it was a bit funny, you changing everything around at the last minute like that. Seemed all right to me as it was.'

'Yes, so did it to me,' Davina agreed feelingly. She should have guessed, she supposed. No one else would have the effrontery, the nerve, to take such a high-handed action. Well, this was just too much. No one could be expected to take something like this lying down. Of all the bare-faced nerve! Davina wished she had Max here so that she could tell him what she thought of him right now.

The whistle blew for a foul as the crowd roared and Davina looked up to see one of the Rovers on the ground. She grabbed her bag and jumped up to go to him, but Mike held her back. 'Wait a minute, he might get up by himself.'

Luckily the player did and she was able to relax again, but shortly before the final whistle another Rovers player, Roger Maynard, was sent flying and this time rolled on the ground in agony. Davina ran out to him, her fair hair flying about her head in the soft breeze, and the whistles and catcalls from the crowd suddenly became deafening again. She wiped the player's face with a sponge soaked in refreshing eau-de-cologne while she talked to him, but he had received a bad kick on the knee and couldn't play on, so she offered to get a stretcher for him, but he insisted on walking off, so Davina helped him up and he put an arm round her shoulder, letting her take most of his weight as he limped off the field. There was another roar and the fans sitting near the team's entrance made some choice remarks as they passed, so that Davina's cheeks were burning by the time they got to the therapy room.

The player saw her face as she helped him on to the treatment couch and said, 'You don't want to take any notice of them.' But he was far more interested in his injury than in the crowd's reaction. 'God,' he groaned, 'I hope I haven't done the cartilage in again. That's all I need!'

'Have you had trouble with it before?'

'Yes, a couple of years ago. It put me out of action for most of the season.'

Davina touched the knee experimentally, her small fingers light and gentle, careful not to cause him any further pain. 'I think it will be all right. So long as I give it the proper treatment straight away and you don't try to use it too quickly.' She got to work, taking off his boot and sock and washing his leg first before she started to treat it.

As she did so the door was pushed open and Max came in. 'How is it?' he demanded abruptly.

Remembering how he'd moved her room around, Davina looked up at him antagonistically, but Max's only interest was in the player.

'Davy says she thinks it'll be okay,' Roger Maynard answered, but added glumly, 'It hurts like hell.'

Both men looked at her distrustfully and Davina felt compelled to justify herself by saying, 'I don't guarantee it, but if I treat it at once it will probably be all right in a few weeks.'

'So why don't you get started, then?'

Davina's eyes flashed angrily, but she bit back the retort that came to her lips and turned back to Roger Maynard. It was obvious that Max had no intention of leaving, so she had to work while he watched her. Using her skill and the equipment she had at her disposal, she worked assiduously on the injured knee, gauging how much to give it, how much movement it could take. She worked for half an hour, aware all the time of Max's brooding presence as he leant against the wall, watching her every move. Mike and the trainer also looked in, saw she was concentrating on her task, and went away again.

At last she straightened up and eased her aching shoulders. 'That's all I can do for it now, but I'll be able to work on it longer tomorrow and then twice a day after that. At the moment it's too sore to take any more. How does it feel?'

'Not as bad as it was,' said Roger, with hope in his voice again.

'Good. I'll bandage it up and you're not to put any weight on it for two days. I'll give you some crutches; you know how to use them, don't you?'

He nodded grimly. 'I've had plenty of practice.'

'Now how about getting home? I suppose you drove here?' He nodded and she said, 'I'll take you home as soon as I've checked on the other players.'

Max spoke for the first time since she had begun the treatment. 'That won't be necessary; I'll drive him home. Do you have a wheelchair to take him out to the car-park?'

She shook her head. 'No. If you remember, you didn't think a wheelchair was necessary,' she pointed out bitingly, trying to keep a note of triumph out of her voice. To win a victory out of something like that was not only undignified but entirely wrong in front of an injured player.

Max shot her a look but said calmly, 'Then we'll use a stretcher. I'll go and arrange it.'

He went out, while Davina put a tube of stretch bandage carefully over Roger's knee. 'Is your wife at home?' she asked him. 'Shall I phone her and tell her you're on your way?'

Shaking his head, the player answered bleakly, 'There's no need. She won't be there. She's staying with her mother at the moment.'

From his tone it was obvious that everything wasn't well at home, so Davina didn't push it. Straightening up, she said, 'I'll just go and check that no one else needs me, then I'll see you home.'

She ran over to the changing-room door, banged on it, and had a hasty word with Mike Douglas, who came to open it. 'Do any of the

other players need me?' she asked. 'I want to see
Roger Maynard safely home.'

'How is he?' asked Mike.

'I think he'll be all right with rest and
treatment.'

He looked glum. 'I hope so; he's a good player.
No, we're all right here. Off you go, girl. Here, you
can take his gear with you.'

When she got back to the therapy room Max
had arrived with a stretcher carried by two St John
Ambulance men. They lifted Roger gently on to it,
and Davina followed carrying a pair of crutches
and Roger's bag. Max was waiting outside with his
Rolls, an ideal car to take the injured man home in
as it had lots of leg room in the back. They got
him in safely, but Max raised his eyebrows when
he saw Davina about to get in beside him. 'Are
you coming, too?'

'Yes, please. I'd like to make sure he's
comfortable at home.'

He nodded, and they set off with Roger giving
directions from the back seat. It hadn't occurred
to Davina that he might live far away, but it took
them nearly half an hour to reach his house,
although Max did drive as smoothly as possible to
make sure his knee didn't get bumped. When they
arrived there was still the problem of getting
Roger out of the car, but Max solved this by
simply picking him up and carrying him inside and
straight up to the bedroom, which said a lot for
Max's strength, because Roger was no lightweight.
Davina waited outside while Max helped him to
change out of his football clothes into pyjamas,
and when she went back in he was lying on the top
of the bed, looking very pale. She had already

given him some painkillers at the stadium but now gave him a couple more. 'I'll leave the bottle with you in case you need them,' she told him, looking at him rather anxiously. 'But you really must rest for the next two days. Isn't there anyone else who can look after you?'

'We could get a professional nurse to come and stay,' Max offered, and Davina guessed that Roger must have confided in him.

Roger hesitated, then said, 'If you could arrange for someone to come during the day. I'll be all right at night.'

Max went downstairs to phone a nursing agency and Davina sat with him until Max came back. 'The nurse will be along in less than an hour,' he informed them.

'I'll stay with Roger till she comes,' Davina volunteered at once. 'I can get a bus back to the stadium.'

'We'll both stay.'

But Roger said in a husky but decisive voice, 'Thanks, but if you don't mind, I'd quite like to be on my own for a while. You can leave the front door on the latch for the nurse.'

Davina hesitated, not liking to leave him on his own, but Max said, 'Yes, of course.' So after making sure that there was nothing more he needed, they left, although it pulled at Davina's heart-strings to leave him lying there looking so fed-up and lonely.

'I could wait down here until the nurse comes.' Davina hung back, reluctant to leave the man she thought of as her patient. 'She might get lost or something.'

'He'll be all right. He has a phone beside his bed

and I've given him the number of the nursing agency.' Max put a firm hand under her elbow and marched her back to his car, opening the passenger door for her.

It was only then that Davina remembered about his high-handed rearrangement of her therapy room. Stiffly, she said, 'Thank you, but I prefer to take a bus.'

Max's eyebrows rose. 'What on earth for?'

'Because I prefer to, that's all.'

An exasperated look came into his eyes. 'For heaven's sake don't start becoming female on me! If you've got something to say then say it.'

'All right, if that's what you want.' Davina faced him antagonistically. 'If you want to know, I think the way you rearranged my therapy room without even bothering to consult me about it was both ill-mannered and autocratic. *And* also unnecessary. *And* I resent it—very much,' she finished feelingly.

'Is that it? I suppose I should have known. Presumably it hasn't occurred to you to ask me why I did it.'

'You did it for no other reason than that you decided you liked it better that way, of course,' she retorted spiritedly.

'Well, you're wrong, but I don't intend to stand here on the pavement arguing about it. Will you please get in the car?' he said shortly, his face becoming angry.

'I've already told you I prefer to . . .'

'To take a bus. Yes, I heard you. But if you'll behave like the adult woman you're supposed to be I'll willingly tell you why I moved it around.'

Davina glared at him for a moment, wanting to tell him to go to hell, but glanced around her and realised that both they and the Rolls were objects of interest from behind a dozen net curtains in the respectable suburban street. 'Oh, very well,' she agreed acidly, and let him shut the door after her as she got in the passenger seat.

Max sat down beside her and started the car, although there was little difference in the noise level from the quietly purring engine. He drove out of the tree-lined avenue and into the main road before saying, 'I realised only this morning that you hadn't left enough space in your room for a stretcher to be brought in and laid beside the couch. So I told one of the men to clear a space. He went too far, admittedly, and I presume that's what you're so angry about, but I didn't have time to stand there and check what he did.'

'Well, you should have made time,' Davina said forcibly. 'Or better still, have got in touch with me so that I could do it.'

'You admit, then, that it was badly arranged,' he said with a sneer.

Trust a man to turn defence into attack! Davina's eyes glittered angrily; she could have explained that she had never had to deal with stretcher cases before, but she was sure Max would only look down on her even more if she tried to make excuses for herself. 'I admit that it needed more space in the centre of the room,' she flashed back. 'But that doesn't excuse the fact that you didn't bother to consult me about it.'

'I tried, but you weren't at the stadium. So I went ahead and made good your mistake. Did you seriously expect me to wait around just so as not to offend your feminine sensitivities?' he demanded sarcastically.

High spots of angry colour appeared in Davina's cheeks as she retorted, 'No, I don't expect you to care about anyone's feelings, especially a woman's.'

She was thrown against her safety belt as Max swerved into the kerb and jerked on the brakes. 'Just what is that supposed to mean?' he demanded fiercely.

Suddenly she remembered his reaction to that kind of remark before and realised that she was close to a confrontation she was bound to lose. She should have remembered earlier, been on her guard. His anger seemed to fill the car, to overwhelm her. 'I only meant that you should have known I . . .' She broke off, aware that she was sinking into pathos, then shook her head and said stiffly, 'It doesn't matter.'

Max's hands tightened on the steering wheel. 'I tried to find you, but you weren't there,' he said harshly.

She lifted her head to look at him, instinctively aware that the atmosphere in the car had changed. Now it was the same as it had been between them when they had danced; the air filled with a kind of electricity, charged with sexual awareness. A muscle at the corner of Max's mouth moved and she thought he was going to say something, but he suddenly turned and began to drive on again, his mouth closed into a grim tight line. Davina, too, sat back in the wide, comfortable seat and watched the road ahead, but she didn't see it; she was aware only of the man beside her and knew that he was just as aware of her. Some kind of chemistry had exploded between them, and now she could only wonder which one of them resented it most.

Back at the stadium, Max parked the car in his reserved parking place. Davina said a stiff, 'Thank you,' and got out before he could come round and open the door for her, then hurried to the therapy room to get it back into some sort of order.

Mike Douglas came in shortly after to enquire about Roger and found her trying to lug her desk back into place. 'You should know better than that,' he scolded. 'Why didn't you get one of the men to help you?'

'They're all busy clearing up the ground. And anyway, I felt like doing something energetic.'

'Did you now? Max Blair been having a go at you again, has he?' Mike asked shrewdly as he helped to move the desk.

'Something like that,' Davina admitted, realising it must be common knowledge around the Club. 'Is he like that with anyone else?'

'He's got a pretty sharp tongue if he sees someone doing anything stupid, but there's always a reason and it doesn't last. What else do you want moved?'

'The treatment couch, please. But his anger does last with me. Do you know why, Mike?'

The trainer shook his head as they lifted the couch back to where Davina wanted it. 'No idea. Perhaps he just doesn't like the idea of a female physio. Anything else?'

'The exercise bicycle can go here, and the rowing machine will have to go over there, nearer the wall.' She looked round, 'There, that should satisfy even Max.' She turned to Mike. 'I think it's something more than that. It has to be.' She hesitated, wondering whether to tell Mike about Max's anger when she'd demanded to know what he'd got against women, but decided against it; it was difficult to explain and somehow seemed like gossiping behind Max's back. Not that he deserved any better from her.

They began to talk about Roger, and Davina tentatively mentioned about the nurse.

'I know; Max told me,' Mike answered. 'Looks like Roger's got some trouble with his wife.'

'But surely she ought to be told that he's been injured. She might not know.'

'He's not so badly injured that he can't call her and tell her himself, if he wants to.' Mike shook his head. 'I don't like interfering between husband and wife.'

'But isn't there anything you can do? I hated leaving him there on his own.'

Mike gave her an amused look. 'Soft-hearted, are you? No, better let him sort it out on his own. If he wants our help he can always ask for it.'

Davina didn't agree with him, but she had to leave it there. She changed out of her track-suit into ordinary clothes after tidying up the rest of the room and then made her way out of the Club, intending to catch the bus home. The fans had all left an hour ago and the car park was almost empty of cars, including Max's Rolls, most of the space being taken up with the refuse collection vehicles waiting to take away the vast amounts of rubbish the fans had left behind. But as she walked towards the main gates someone called her name, and Davina turned to see Giles Allinson waving to her from his car. She walked over and he got out.

'How's Roger?' he asked.

'Not too bad. With luck he'll be okay in about three weeks.'

'That's great. I was just leaving. Would you like a lift?'

Davina smiled at him. 'You don't know which way I'm going.'

He grinned in return. 'No, I don't, do I? But it doesn't matter; I'm in no hurry. I'll take you wherever you want to go.'

She wasn't sure whether she wanted to accept a lift from him or not. 'It's a nice car,' she temporised.

He was immediately enthusiastic, and Davina felt as if she'd turned on a verbal tap as he poured out a technical description of his silver sports car. 'You must come for a ride in her,' he finished insistently. 'You'll see what I mean.'

'Well, I don't know.' She glanced at her watch. 'I don't have that much time.'

'Just ten minutes and then I'll take you straight home,' Giles urged.

It was hard to refuse in the face of such insistence and Davina didn't want to hurt his feelings, so she nodded and said, 'Okay, just ten minutes, then.'

It was a neat little two-seater sports car with a long sloping bonnet and a mid-engine which gave it great balance, but Giles wasn't a good driver. She found that out almost as soon as they'd started off. He drove on his brakes instead of his engine, accelerating too fast from traffic lights and pulling up with a jerk instead of slowing to a stop. Possibly he was trying to impress her, but it had the opposite effect; Davina didn't much care for being thrown about in her seat and having to brace herself against the dashboard. But Giles didn't seem to notice. He drove up to the dual carriageway and put his foot down, overtaking the other cars until he was breaking the speed limit.

'Is that a police siren I can hear?' Davina remarked, and was relieved to see that he immediately slowed down, looking in his mirror.

'I can't see one.'

'Oh, good. I must have been mistaken. How embarrassing, though, if we'd been stopped.'

He grinned. 'Yes, I suppose so, but it's difficult to keep down to the silly limit they set in this country. They ought to have the same rules here as in Germany, where you do what speed you like on the motorways.'

Davina didn't entirely agree with him, not the way he drove, but she let it pass. 'I'm afraid I'll have to get home now,' she told him.

'If you like we could take a run out into the country and have a meal somewhere.'

'Thanks, but I really must get back. I've promised to babysit tonight.'

'Okay, then.' His voice regretful, Giles turned back towards Redford. 'Can you drive?'

'I've got a licence, but I don't possess a car yet.'

'Perhaps I'll let you drive this one day,' Giles offered generously.

Davina would have liked to get her hands on the car, but not with Giles sitting next to her sweating buckets of apprehension in case she crashed it, so she put him out of his misery. 'Oh, I'm quite sure I could never drive it like you do. And I'm rather out of practice.'

'Why don't you buy yourself a car?' he asked.

'Maybe I will when I've saved enough money, but I can get around all right by public transport.'

They chatted on and pulled up with the usual

jerk at the main traffic lights in the town, Giles's too heavy foot still on the accelerator so that the engine raced while the brake was on as he waited impatiently for the lights to change. There was a car on the inside of them, a big car whose driver was looking down at them. Davina glanced at the driver, then did a stunned double-take and looked again—into Max's angrily frowning face.

She managed a feeble nod of recognition, but Max was looking past her at Giles, who was blissfully unaware of him. Max's frown deepened and he shot her a look that spoke volumes, and she already knew every word off by heart. It accused her of having used her job to get to know the players, just as he'd said she would. And there was a menace in his frown that promised her that she hadn't heard the last of it. The lights changed to amber and they were immediately away with a roar, and for once Davina was glad of Giles's speed as they pulled away from Max's silent but scorching anger.

CHAPTER FOUR

DAVINA had a little difficulty shaking Giles off
when they drew up outside the flat, as he asked if
he could come babysitting with her. 'Good
heavens, you'd be bored stiff!' she exclaimed.

'No more than I would be on my own. I don't
know anyone in this town except you and the
other players. The Club found some digs for me
and they're not bad, but I don't want to sit there
watching the television with the landlady every
night.'

'And I suppose you don't know any girls? Look,
how about if I arranged a foursome next
Saturday? I'm going out with my boy-friend then
and I'll bring a girl-friend along for you to meet.'

'You've already got a boy-friend, then?'

''Fraid so. Would you like to come out with us
next Saturday?'

Giles agreed, making the best of it, and Davina
was at last free to go in and get herself a meal. But
when she looked in the fridge she found that her
appetite had gone. It had disappeared somewhere
about the time when she had looked up and found
herself staring into Max's face. Oh, darn! She
dropped into an armchair, feeling miserable and
depressed. What had started out to be just an
innocent joyride would probably end up as yet
another misdeed for Max to carry to his Board,
yet another reason to back his argument that she
should be got rid of.

And this thing that had sprung up between them, this chemical awareness? Davina was feminine enough to wonder if Max would change his mind because of that and let her stay on, but she came to the conclusion that he would do just the opposite, that it would make him even more determined to see her gone. She got up and moved restlessly around the flat, trying to put it out of her mind but not succeeding. Nothing quite like this had ever happened to her before, not discovering such animosity against her, nor this electric spark that she and Max struck against one another, and she had no idea how to fight either of them. The best way seemed to be to avoid Max as much as possible, but when she had the bad luck to draw up beside him at a traffic light it did rather seem that the fates were against her. Davina sighed frustratedly, then saw the time and hurriedly made herself a sandwich, eating it in the bath so that she wouldn't be late.

Bill came to pick her up and she spent an uneventful evening looking after their children, and after they'd gone to bed, watching the TV and knitting herself a pair of leg-warmers to wear under her track-suit in the winter. The Buckleys came back about midnight and, to Davina's surprise, Anne offered to run her home instead of Bill. But it seemed that Anne had a reason: on the way she said offhandedly, 'I ran into an old school friend of mine last week. We were both looking at clothes in that new boutique that's opened in the precinct.'

'Is it any good?' Davina asked idly, tired and not really listening.

'Not bad—their casuals are good. But to get

back to this friend; she happens to be a niece of one of the Rovers' Directors. Well, we got talking and I happened to mention Maxwell Blair.'

Davina's tiredness suddenly left her as her feminine nose scented scandal. 'Oh, really?' she said just as casually.

'Mm. It seems the Club did a thorough check into his background before admitting him to the Board, and they naturally enquired about his wife.' She paused to let that sink in, then went on, 'They found out that his wife was dead.'

'Dead!' Davina swung round to face her, all pretence at uninterest forgotten.

'Yes. She was killed in a car crash about three years ago.'

'So *that's* why he ... But no, it doesn't explain why Max ...' Davina was talking to herself, her thoughts in a whirl.

'Why Max what?' probed Anne. 'What doesn't it explain?'

'What? Oh, his attitude. Surely he can't be against all women because his wife was killed. That doesn't make sense. Unless it was a woman driver who killed his wife. Was it, do you know?'

Anne shook her head. 'No, she went into a lorry. It was her own fault. Is Max very anti, then? He didn't look as if he hated women at the dance.'

'No, that's true. But he's very anti me for some reason.'

Davina sighed, thinking of Roger Maynard, alone because his wife had left him, and of Max, alone because his wife had been torn from him. And then there was even Giles Allinson, his ambition leaving him alone and friendless in a new city. Three men who didn't deserve to be lonely.

She pulled herself together, realising that she was becoming maudlin. They were men, they didn't need her pity, especially Max. Whereas the other two men might accept sympathy and use it—in fact Giles had tried to create it in her—Max never would, she was certain of that. Even though he was so nasty to her, she knew that he was more of a man than the other two would ever be.

The next day was Sunday, and Bill gave her a lift over to the Club where she collected her spare Interferaction machine and then dropped her off with it at Roger Maynard's house. The nurse opened the door for them and Bill carried the heavy machine upstairs, staying to have a few words with Roger and a look at his knee before going off to take his children out. But first he gave Davina a nod of approval that told her she was doing the right thing.

Roger's knee wasn't so sore today, so she was able to work on it longer and left the house over an hour later, then had to stand for nearly as long while she waited for a bus to take her home. In the evening she made the same journey again to give his leg another session of treatment.

This time the nurse had gone home and Davina let herself in with the latch key given her the previous evening. Roger was lying on top of the bed again, watching a film on television, the remains of a meal on a tray on the bedside table. 'Hallo. How's it going?' she asked cheerfully.

He looked at her glumly. 'I'm sick to death of lying here. I've read all the papers and there's nothing worth watching on the box.'

'Never mind. You should be able to move about a bit tomorrow,' Davina encouraged.

He turned off the TV and they talked while she worked on his leg, but she found that they had little in common. During the conversation, though, he found out that she could drive and offered to lend her his car, which was still parked outside the Rovers' ground. 'You might as well use it; it doesn't look as if I'll be driving for a while.'

'Sooner than you think. There, that's it for today, I think. Thanks for the loan of the car. Is there anything I can get you?'

'I'd like some more magazines and a few beers. And perhaps you could get me some stamps and a few pounds of apples.'

In the end it came to quite a list and Davina could see it all taking up a good hour or two of her time, but she would probably save that with the use of the car.

She went home feeling tired, but was up early the next morning to go to the Club and collect Roger's car and then do his shopping before she went to his house again. He was grateful for the things she had brought, but had had a restless night and seemed to have spent most of it thinking of more things that he wanted done, judging from the list he gave her. Twice a day for the rest of that week, Davina went to his home to treat his knee, and by the end of it she felt as if she was his personal dogsbody. Because he had lent her his car Roger seemed to think he had the right to ask her to do all his errands, from taking his laundry to buying his food, and all this on top of doing her work at the Club and running her own home.

By Friday Davina began to feel it was vitally necessary for Roger's wife to come home, for her sake as well as his. Like most men, Roger hated to be incapacitated and was a restless and unwilling patient, so Davina decided to phone Anne and make a few enquiries. Between them, they managed to find out the address where Roger's wife was staying, but reluctantly decided that they couldn't just phone her and ask her to come home as this would give her an advantage over Roger. They wondered what a little jealousy might do. With a lot of rather guilty giggling, the two girls got together and composed a letter to Roger's wife. After many false starts their final draft read: 'Did you know that a woman comes to your husband every night?' and was signed, 'A well-wisher'. They had been going to sign it 'A good neighbour', but Davina objected in case Roger's wife accused any of the people living nearby. Even now she looked at it dubiously. 'We can't possibly send it, Anne. We might get arrested for sending poison pen letters or something!'

'I don't see how when you're talking about yourself,' the older woman answered reasonably. 'And you want his wife to come home, don't you?'

'Definitely,' Davina agreed feelingly. 'He's a terrible patient. The nurse has been cancelled now that he's getting around on crutches and he's running me off my feet!'

'Well, send the letter, then. Or else try and persuade him to phone her himself.'

'I've tried loads of times already, both directly and indirectly, but he won't budge. He says *she* left and so she's got to be the one to make the first move. But it's obvious he wants her back. Stubborn fool!'

'All men are stubborn fools,' said Anne, with a

wealth of experience in her tone. 'We'll have to think of something else, then.'

But they got talking about other things, and Davina went home to have an early night before the away match tomorrow with the problem still unresolved.

The Rovers' first away match of the season was to be played in Wolverhampton in the Midlands and the coach was leaving at ten-thirty in the morning from the ground. Aware of her last unfortunate encounter with Max, Davina got there early, carrying a bag with a clean track-suit in it, and went down to the therapy room to collect everything she would need to take with her. During her first couple of weeks at the Club she had interviewed each of the players and filled in the record cards of their past injuries, and these she put in her bag with all the other equipment she would need. As she did so, carefully checking through her list, there was a brief rap on the door and Max walked in. She stood up to face him defensively, wondering if he had reported her to the Board and had come to tell her to leave, an announcement she had half been waiting for all week.

His face was cold, but she had expected that anyway, and his voice was as chilling as the air outside as he said, 'Good morning.'

'Good morning,' Davina managed to answer as steadily as she could, her hands nervously pleating the piece of paper she held behind her.

'How is Maynard's knee?'

She told him in detail, but halfway through became aware that he wasn't really listening and guessed that he had already seen Roger for himself. His eyes seemed to be fixed on her face, watchful and slightly sardonic, so that she became nervous and her voice died in her throat.

'Go on,' he sneered, his voice still icy.

'That's all really. I hope he'll be fit enough to play again in a couple of weeks or so.'

'Can't you be more definite?'

'No. He's had an injury on that knee before and if it's hurried he could do permanent damage to it.'

Max nodded. 'Very well.' He looked over at the things she had collected together. 'Are these what you're taking to the match?'

'Yes.'

'Do you have a check list?' She nodded and he held out his hand. 'Let me see it.'

Davina made an instinctive move to obey him, then stopped. 'Why?' she asked.

His left eyebrow rose and she felt the pulse begin to beat in her throat. 'Because I want to check it for myself.'

'But that's my job,' she said firmly. '*And* I'm quite capable of doing it without supervision.'

'In between running after the unmarried players, presumably,' Max bit back, his voice heavy with contempt. '*And* just as I predicted.'

Her face tightening, Davina said shortly, 'Giles Allinson was kind enough to offer me a lift home last Saturday.'

'Really? How strange, then, that when I saw you you were driving *towards* the ground.' He saw her cheeks start to flush and said scathingly, 'Quite.'

'It was just a ride home,' she repeated, not seeing why she should have to go into details.

'Do I take it that you won't be seeing him again?' Max asked smoothly.

Davina was about to say no, but remembered their foursome later that night. She hesitated, and Max immediately picked her up.

'So you are seeing him again!'

'I didn't say that.'

'You didn't have to. You'll have to learn not to let your feelings show in your face if you want to succeed in your crafty little game. Not that I intend to let you succeed here.'

Her chin came up defiantly. 'What I do in my own time is my business! It's nothing to do with you.'

'It is when you start distracting the players. I've warned you about keeping away from them and I shan't warn you again. Just try remembering that you're only here on sufferance.'

'If you intend to get rid of me anyway, there doesn't seem to be much point in obeying your— your dictates, does there?' Davina retorted, her hands curling into tight balls of suppressed emotion.

Max's jaw tightened and he opened his mouth to make a scathing retort, but bit it back when the door opened and Mike Douglas came in. Mike looked at their stormy faces and said diplomatically, 'Er—the coach has arrived. Anything you want me to help you carry, Davy?'

She turned to him gratefully. 'Thanks, Mike. If you could take that box, I can manage the rest.'

'Right you are. Let's go, then.'

Davina picked up her bag of equipment and followed him out to the waiting coach. Most of the players were already inside and there was an empty seat next to Giles, but she deliberately went to sit by herself. Several of the Directors were going to the match, and Davina was surprised to see that they, too, were travelling up on the coach; she somehow hadn't expected them to travel with the players but to have gone in a couple of limousines. Max was among them, but he sat quite a few rows behind her on the other side of the coach. Mike got on after seeing her gear into the luggage bay and came to sit beside her, so that she was doubly grateful to him and greeted him with a warm smile. They chatted for about half an hour and then he moved on to talk to one of the players.

His action seemed to give others the same idea and there was a general movement as people changed places. Giles, rather unfortunately in the circumstances, took the opportunity to come and ask Davina about the arrangements for that evening. She answered him with a show of cheerfulness, but was uncomfortably aware of Max's eyes on her back. An almost overwhelming urge to turn round and look at him grew in her, but she managed to control it until the coach drew into a service area on the motorway and they were free to go in to the restaurant for a coffee. She couldn't help looking at Max then and was relieved to see that he was deep in conversation with Sir Reginald, the Chairman. Deciding to hurry off the coach, she reached up to the rack to pick up her bag and gave an involuntary exclamation. 'Oh no!'

Giles turned to look at her. 'What is it?'

'My sports bag with my track-suit in it; I've left it behind in the therapy room,' she told him in

dismay. 'Now what am I going to do? I can't go
on to the field like this!' And she gestured to her
sweater, skirt and high-heeled sandals.

'No, I suppose you can't,' Giles agreed, and
began to laugh.

Davina frowned at him. 'It's not funny.' She
knew quite well why she had forgotten the bag, of
course; it was because she had had that clash with
Max just before they had left; it had completely
thrown her. And if I appear on the field without a
track-suit, he'll really be down on me like a ton of
bricks, she thought despairingly.

'Cheer up,' Giles told her. 'You can borrow
mine.'

'But won't you need it while you're warming
up?'

'I think I'll be able to survive without it.'

'Oh, *thanks,* Giles! I really appreciate it.'

He laughed and gave her a mock leer as they
moved out of their seats. 'For you, darling,
anything.'

She laughed in return, much relieved, and joined
in the game by raising her eyebrows and saying
throatily, 'Is that a promise, darling?' then glanced
over her shoulder and realised that Max was just
behind her and had heard!

The Rovers won the match and there weren't
any injuries, but they were the only good things
about it as far as Davina was concerned. She was
glad to get back to the ground at last that evening,
although she had to drive over to Roger's to give
him his treatment before she could change to go
out.

As she inserted her key in Roger's door it was
suddenly jerked open and, to Davina's surprise,

she found herself face to face with a very angry young woman. 'Oh! Hallo,' she said inadequately.

Roger's anxious face appeared behind the woman's shoulder as he hopped into the hall on his crutches. 'Hallo, Davy,' he said quickly. 'This is my wife, Karen. I was just telling her you were about due.'

'He says you're the physio from the Club,' Karen said in a disbelieving tone.

'Yes, that's right.' Davina stepped into the hall. 'Didn't we meet at the dinner and dance?'

'I wasn't there.'

'Oh, weren't you?' It was obvious that the woman was highly suspicious of her, so she said in as brisk and businesslike way as possible, 'Well, I have to give Roger his treatment and I'm in rather a hurry.'

His wife watched all the time that Davina was working on Roger's leg, and afterwards she more or less demanded the keys of his car, which was inconvenient to say the least and meant that Davina had to phone Peter, her boy-friend, and ask him to come and pick her up. Karen was a little more affable after he arrived, but Davina was glad to leave them to what she hoped was their reconciliation. She didn't know what had brought his wife home, but she sincerely hoped they would make up their differences so that she wouldn't have to run all Roger's errands any more and his wife would be able to bring him into the Club for treatment, which wouls save Davina a lot of time.

That evening she took along her friend Elaine and the four of them had a pleasant time, going first to a restaurant for a meal and then on to a disco. Elaine was thrilled to be with Giles and he

seemed to get on well with Peter, too, although
the two men talked football for quite a lot of the
time, discussing that afternoon's match, which
Peter had seen on the television. Davina was
content to just relax after a long day and wonder if
Max would get to hear about her being out with
Giles. This wasn't the sort of place he was likely to
come to, but Davina was beginning to feel as if he
was fated to learn everything bad about her and
nothing good, like the way he'd looked her up and
down when he'd seen her in Giles's track-suit at
half-time and made it perfectly obvious from the
look he gave her that he knew what she had done.

She sighed, and Peter looked at her enquiringly.
'Anything the matter? You look depressed.'

'Sorry. I was just thinking about work.'

'I thought you liked the job?'

'I do. It's just one of the Directors who has a
down on me.'

'Oh, yes, I remember you told me about him.
Still getting at you, is he? Never mind—forget him.
Come and dance.'

But although Davina tried, she couldn't put
Max completely out of her mind, and she felt no
great surprise when she was summoned to his
office on Monday afternoon. She didn't go
immediately, but took the time to brush her
shining bell of fair hair and to freshen her make-
up. If she had to face him, then she at least wanted
to be confident of looking her best.

Max's office overlooked a practice field at the
back of the stadium. When she knocked and went
in he was standing at the window with his back to
her. He turned, slowly, but the light was behind
him and she couldn't see his face properly. He

didn't speak, so she said, 'You wanted to see me?' trying to keep the nervousness out of her voice.

'Yes.' He crossed to the desk and she could see his face now as he bent to pick up a piece of paper. He was frowning, of course, and Davina, for no reason at all, wondered if he would ever smile at her. He didn't smile a lot, maybe that was because of his wife, but he sometimes smiled at other women, she'd seen him at the dance, although he had never come even close to it with her.

He came round and stood just in front of her, his look accusing, and Davina's heart began to beat faster in trepidation. The paper he held looked like a letter, and she could only think that he had brought the other Directors round to his way of thinking and it was a letter of dismissal. Well, if she was going to go, she sure as hell wasn't going to go out crying. Her chin came up and she gave a defiant toss of her head, her hair swinging into a golden cloud about her face. Max paused, the letter half held towards her, an arrested expression in his eyes as he looked at her. Then he seemed to pull himself together, his jaw tightened and he almost thrust the letter at her. 'Roger Maynard's wife was here today,' he said harshly. 'She showed me this.'

Surprised, Davina took it from him and then stood in appalled shock as she read it. It was the letter she and Anne had jokingly concocted to bring Roger's wife home! Anne must have sent it after all, completely against her own wishes. She didn't know what to do, what to say, but could only stand staring down at the letter.

'Yes, it is nasty, isn't it?' Max said into the silence. 'You can imagine how Mrs Maynard feels.

Obviously one of her neighbours put the wrong interpretation on your visits to the house—a thing that would never have happened if the Board had listened to me and engaged a male physio as usual.'

'Why—why have you shown it to me?' Davina managed hoarsely.

'I thought it right that you should know. Also the police might want to question you about it.'

'The—the police! You're going to show it to the police?' she gasped, feeling faint.

'Of course. Sending poison pen letters is a disgusting petty crime. And Mrs Maynard, of course, wants to know which of her neighbours sent it.'

Davina mentally said goodbye to the best—and shortest—job she'd ever had. 'That won't be necessary. I know who sent it.'

Max's eyes came up to stare into her face. 'Who?' he demanded sharply.

'I did. I sent it,' she added, so that there wouldn't be any doubt.

He looked at her incredulously and then his face grew grim. 'Would you mind telling me why?'

She gave a small shrug. 'His wife had left him and Roger was very unhappy. He wouldn't get in touch with her or even let me tell her that he was injured. It was a case of both of them refusing to make the first move, so I decided to see what a little good old-fashioned jealousy would do. And it worked. She came straight home.' Davina had tried to end on an optimistic note, but one look at Max's thunderous face told her it was no use.

'You had the temerity to go behind Maynard's

back to try and get him and his wife together?' he exclaimed furiously. 'And you decided to use a dirty, contemptuous way like this! What if Mrs Maynard had gone straight to the police instead of coming to me? Can you imagine the scandal it would have caused? The Rovers' name would have been dragged through every gutter press paper in the country. They feed on this kind of thing! And just what right do you think you had to play God like this? It was up to the Maynards to sort out their own problems.'

'How were they supposed to sort them out when they wouldn't even speak to each other?' Davina fired back. 'They could have gone on for ever like that. And anyway, I was ...' She stopped abruptly.

'You were what?' Max demanded sharply. And when she didn't speak, 'There's no point in not telling me now, is there?'

Impossible not to understand what he meant by that. 'All right. Roger lent me his car to get to and from his house when I treated him, but after the nurse left I had to do all his shopping and run all his errands, and I was getting tired of it. I thought it was about time his wife came home and looked after him instead of me. And I thought it was all right to send a letter if it was about yourself,' she finished lamely.

Max's expression slowly changed. He glanced down at the letter again, then tore it up into very small pieces which he dropped into the waste paper basket. 'Don't you have a car?' he asked, going round the desk so that he was half turned away from her.

'No.' Davina's voice was puzzled as she

wondered why he didn't just tell her to go.

'Do you need one to visit Maynard?'

Suddenly hopeful, Davina answered, 'Not if his wife stays with him. She drove him here for treatment today.'

'I see.' He looked down at his desk, then said lightly, 'If you need to visit any of the players at home in future, you may borrow a car from the Club. If you're in difficulties come to me—and don't try to solve them yourself in such a small-minded and underhand way. Do you understand?'

'Yes. Thank you,' she answered on a relieved gasp.

'Don't thank me. My opinion of you hasn't changed. This sordid little incident has only enhanced it.'

Thanking her stars that she was still in a job, Davina took great care to keep out of Max's way during the next few weeks, and this was made much easier when she heard that he had gone away on business. For the first time she was really able to relax and enjoy her job and get to know the players and the rest of the people who worked at the ground without the threat of Max watching her every move.

She began to pick up all the football jargon, to tell a friendly match from a needle match, and to know where the team were placed in the League, the Football Association cup, the European Cup, and all the other tournaments that took place during the busy season. She even began to understand what the players were talking about when they discussed the game after the match, and to know by watching them when the men were playing well and when they weren't.

Roger Maynard's knee responded well to her treatment, especially now that he had made it up with his wife and was happier in himself, and within a month he was back in the team.

The warmth of summer changed to the first chill of autumn and it was pouring with rain when they played their second round match in the F.A. Cup. Luckily it was a home match, but Davina felt really chilly as she sat with a waterproof jacket over her track-suit and wellingtons on her feet. She had to run out on to the pitch two or three times and by the time the match was over had almost as much mud on her as the players. The hurt players managed to carry on, but when it was over she treated the most badly hurt of them first, then went to the changing room to collect her next customer. His leg had seized up and Mike Douglas wasn't around, so she had to go into the room and help him along, turning a blind eye to the men who were still showering or changing. At the end of a gruelling match they were too exhausted to care, and by now they had all got used to her and tended to look on her as a nurse or doctor, which suited Davina very well.

There were several people standing around in the corridor outside, but she took little notice of them as she helped her patient along. Someone opened the door of the therapy room for her, but she was intent on what she was doing and merely murmured her thanks. She worked on the man assiduously, making sure that there was nothing more she could do for him before she strapped up his leg and sent him home with one of the other players. Only then did Davina give any thought to herself. It was warm in the room and she had stripped down to her red and white REDFORD ROVERS printed T-shirt while she worked, but she was still wearing her mud-stained trousers. She was about to slip them off, but remembered in time to go over and lock the door first. But as she reached out to turn the key it was pushed open and Davina had to take a hasty step backwards to get out of the way as Max walked in.

She hadn't known he was back; no one had told her. Her heart gave a crazy kind of jump and then she was immediately on her guard, her body stiffening as she eyed him warily, all the dictatorial lectures she had received from him flooding back into her memory. And it seemed that today was to be no exception. His eyes were bright with anger as Max stepped into the room and shut the door firmly behind him.

For a moment he just glared at her, then said brusquely, 'Just who the hell gave you permission to go into the changing room while the players were taking their showers?'

So that was it. Davina sighed and said, 'No one gave me permission. I didn't ask for it. If I have . . .'

But he didn't let her finish. 'So you just took it on yourself to walk in there and embarrass the players. Just what are you—some kind of female voyeur?' he demanded contemptuously. 'Does it give you a cheap thrill to see a naked man? If you think I'm going to tolerate such behaviour here then you're mistaken! I shall . . .'

It had been a long day; Davina was tired and more than aware of her grubby state. She had been enjoying her job, but now Max had come back to spoil everything again. And she suddenly knew she wasn't going to take it from him any more. Throwing her head back, she suddenly yelled, 'Shut up! How dare you just barge in here and speak to me like that? If I need to go into the changing room to help one of the players, then I'll do it, because it's part of my job. I don't deliberately look at them and they don't care anyway. I'm just the physio to them.'

Max was staring at her as if a brick wall had suddenly become alive, and her heart filled with a glorious rage as she drew herself up and said, 'And I'm just about sick of the way you're forever picking on me. If you want to throw your weight around, then you'll just have to find someone else to act as your doormat, because I've had enough! Everything here went perfectly smoothly while you were away, so why don't you get out and leave me alone to get on with my job?'

She glared at him challengingly, chin thrust forward and bright spots of colour on her cheeks. Her chest, too, was pushed forward beneath the tight-fitting T-shirt, the shape of each firm young breast outlined by the soft material. Her whole attitude was one of belligerent defiance.

Max took a swift step forward and caught hold of her arm, his grip so tight that she winced. His eyes blazing with anger, he jerked her arm roughly, shaking her. 'You little hellcat! Do you know what you're saying?'

'Certainly I do,' she retorted at once. 'You may be as rich as Croesus, but you don't yet own this Club, and you certainly don't own me. I shall say what I want, because my job here is just as important as yours. And I don't give a damn about what you think of me!'

'Don't you, by God!' He spoke with savage fury, his self-control snapping as he pulled her violently against him. For a moment his eyes blazed down into hers, then his head came down and his mouth took hers in a cruel embrace, forcing her head back, his lips hurting her.

There had been those few seconds of warning, but even so it took Davina several moments before she recovered from her stunned surprise and began to struggle. But Max twisted her arm behind her back and put his free hand in her hair, so that she couldn't move without him hurting her. But even so she tried to twist her face away from his, but he pulled her savagely back and she gave a gasp of pain under his mouth. Then she tried to bite him, making him give a, snarl of anger as he arched her body under his, holding her prisoner against him so that she couldn't move at all.

He was free, then, to ravage her mouth as he wished, to kiss her on a growing tide of angry passion—a kiss that devoured her youth and femininity, that took and gave nothing in return. He didn't seek for a response or care whether she gave it or not. He took her mouth with a greedy, savage hunger born out of a suddenly uncontroll-able need that had too long been denied.

Davina gave up trying to physically fight him, but she held herself stiffly in his arms, refusing to open her lips, to give him entry to the inner sanctum of her mouth. She made angry sounds in her throat, swearing at him under her breath, tears of fury in her eyes. It became difficult to breathe and she gave a whimper of distress as her senses began to swim, but still he held her pressed against his hardening body as though he would never let her go.

CHAPTER FIVE

IT was some sound outside in the corridor that finally got to Max and he slowly, reluctantly raised his head. At first he didn't open his eyes, keeping them tightly shut, just as he kept his tight hold on her arm.

Davina gasped, fighting for breath, then wrenched herself furiously out of his grasp, hitting his arm out of the way. His eyes flew open and Max stared down at her, his mouth working as he tried to recover control. 'Davina ...' he began hoarsely, but she rounded on him furiously, the tears of humiliation and anger glistening on her cheeks.

'Get out of here!' she yelled at him. 'Do you hear me? Just get out!'

He half lifted his hand in a pleading gesture, but then his face tightened and he turned and strode quickly out of the room.

The moment the door shut behind him, Davina ran to lock it, then leaned against the wall, shuddering with emotion, feeling used and dirty. Her mouth felt bruised and sore, so after a few minutes she went over to the washbasin and looked at herself in the mirror there. Like every normal girl, Davina had read reports of rape in the papers and wondered with a cold shudder what it must be like, but now she felt that in some small part she knew, for what Max had done to her mouth had been no less than rape; the only

mitigating circumstance the fact that he hadn't
wanted to, that some inner compulsion triggered
off by his anger at her defiance, had made him act
the way he did. And now he was probably hating
himself as much as he hated her. She ran the cold
water tap and slowly washed her face, then
suddenly felt that she had to get away from here,
so she quickly changed and bundled her things
into her holdall, then ran out of the building,
longing for the open air again.

It was still raining, Davina realised that she'd
left her umbrella behind, but there was no way she
was going back for it. She said a brisk good night
to the doorman and ran down the steps at the
entrance, putting up her collar against the rain.
There was a long queue at the bus stop that
extended past the shelter, the people outside
grumbling because the buses were running late and
getting there full. A woman offered to let her share
her umbrella, but Davina shook her head and
began to walk. Maybe she could get a bus in the
town centre, or even find a taxi.

She was walking into the rain, the wind sending
it hurtling against her face so that it was difficult
to see. And the black skies had brought an early
night so that the cars that went by already had
their lights on and the houses she passed had
drawn their curtains to shut out the wintry
weather. There weren't many people about; she
passed a small group who had got off a bus on the
other side of the road, and who hurried off to their
homes, and then she was alone again, her head
down against the wind.

A car went by, then drew into the kerb, but she
didn't take any notice until a voice said her name

and then she stopped and looked round, her hand up to her throat, holding her collar together. It was Max in his Rolls. He had wound down the electric window on the passenger side and was leaning towards her, his face lit by the street lamp. 'Get in,' he said harshly. 'I'll take you home.'

But she could tell by his face that he didn't want to; that he was only doing it because he felt he had to.

'No.' She shook her head and began to hurry on again.

He drove up beside her again and this time Max began to get out of the car. Davina looked desperately round and saw a bus coming up to a stop about a hundred yards behind her. She began to run, waving her arm, and to her relief the driver stopped and let her push her way on. 'Just about got room for a skinny one,' he said cheerfully as she gave him her fare. Then he drove on, overtaking Max's Rolls which was still parked at the kerb. 'Look at that!' the driver laughed. 'Looks as if his Roller's broken down.'

Davina glanced out into the street and saw Max still standing by his car. Their eyes met in a scorching glance through the rain-splashed window, and then the bus had driven by and he was lost in the darkness.

The Redford Rovers were having a good season; so far they had won all their home matches and most of their aways, drawing some of the others. Mike Douglas laughingly told Davina they were thinking of adopting her as their lucky mascot, which gave her a warm glow of wellbeing. She got on well with the players, especially since she'd got

Roger Maynard back on the field so quickly, and they looked forward to seeing her warm smile on their bench even on the most depressing days. And Davina was happy so long as she didn't run into Max. He didn't seem to come to the Club so often, which was a help, but he was nearly always in the coach when they travelled to an away game. Luckily he seemed to want to avoid her as much as she did him, so it was easy to sit at opposite ends of the coach and make sure he was well out of the way before she got off herself.

In November she received official notification that she had been put on the permanent staff, which gave her a dizzy feeling of triumph and security. So much for Max Blair and his threats! She took Peter out to celebrate, the first time they'd been out as a twosome for quite some time. Usually they went with Giles and Elaine at weekends, and during the week Peter and Giles had got into the habit of playing snooker at a local club, so Davina seldom saw him alone. It suited her; she didn't want to get serious, and luckily Peter felt the same, so she didn't feel at all guilty about continuing to see him.

At the beginning of December the team had to go to Bristol to play an away match and as it was such a long distance, it was decided to stay at a hotel overnight rather than travel back the same day. The team chalked up yet another win and decided to have an impromptu party to celebrate. The hotel provided them with a room and a disco, and the kitchen even promised to come up with a late supper. For guests they invited all the losing team and their club officials and anyone any of them knew who lived in the area. Giles had warned Davina that a party was on the cards, so she had taken a dress with her, a rather stunning red one with shoestring straps that tied on the shoulders and a slinky skirt that flared at the bottom six inches.

They had dinner first in the hotel restaurant, Davina sharing a table with Giles, Mike Douglas and Roger Maynard, and they didn't go in to the party until gone nine. Davina had felt a little nervous about going at all if Max was to be there, but Mike mentioned that he had been invited out to dinner by one of the local Directors, so she was able to go along in happy anticipation of a good evening.

Most of the opposing team brought girls along with them, but Davina found herself much in demand as the only female with the Rovers side. She was danced almost literally off her feet until after supper when some of the girls on the hotel staff were willingly allowed to gatecrash the party. Things began to get pretty hectic then as the music really warmed up and everyone let their hair down. Somebody put on an old-fashioned rock'n' roll record and she and Giles tried to dance to it as they'd seen their parents' generation in the old films, waving their arms in the air or holding each other at arm's length as they jived to the compulsive beat.

When the music ended at last they fell into each other's arms, exhausted, and collapsing with laughter.

'My God, how did they keep that up all night?' gasped Giles. 'I'm worn out already—and I'm supposed to be fit!'

'It's all this high living,' Davina gasped, clinging

to his arm. 'Didn't you know—we're the degenerate generation.'

Giles laughed. 'I like that! Come on, let's get even more degenerate. I need another drink after that!'

They staggered laughingly towards the bar, their arms round each other's waists, but Davina's steps faltered even more when she saw Max standing nearby, watching them, his mouth twisted sardonically. She tried to look away and ignore him, but Giles had had enough to drink to make him a little reckless. 'Hi, Max,' he called out. 'Glad to see you could make it. Have a drink with us?'

Davina tugged his arm agitatedly, but it was too late; Max gave him a rather guarded look, then nodded. 'Thank you. I'll have a whisky and soda.'

He moved over to stand beside her as Giles went to get the drinks, but Davina couldn't look at him, let alone find anything to say. She looked round the room, at Giles's back, down at her hands, anywhere but at Max.

Into the heavy silence, he said caustically, 'You seem to be enjoying yourself.'

She gripped her hands together, her eyes fixed on the little silver ring her grandmother had given her, her heart beating as fast as the music as she remembered the last time they'd been alone together. 'Yes. It—it's fun.'

'And you seem to be getting on well with Giles.'

She nodded, willing to agree to that, until she realised what Max was implying. Her head came up swiftly then as she was immediately on the defensive. But the look she was expecting to see on his face wasn't there. Instead she surprised an expression almost of wistfulness, of yearning.

There was bleakness in his eyes and a sad curve to his thin mouth. For a moment Davina's eyes widened in surprise, but then she guessed he must be thinking about his wife and looked quickly away, feeling helpless in the face of his grief.

'Davina.'

'Yes.' She raised reluctant eyes to look at him.

Max was gazing earnestly down at her, and again she had that strange sensation that they were alone in the room. He frowned, as if he found it difficult to find words, and began to speak just as Giles came back. Max immediately broke off and turned to the other man, asking him his opinion of the afternoon's match as he took his drink from him.

Davina had got used to football talk going on around her by now, but she didn't appreciate being ignored as Max encouraged Giles to go on talking about the game. Her mind rebelled and so did her heart. She didn't want to stand here near Max, or to be aware of the growing tension as they both listened politely to Giles without either of them really hearing him. Max turned slightly so that he was facing her, his grey eyes fixed intently on her face even when he was drinking from his glass or nodding at something Giles said. The air between them seemed to crackle with electricity, like a fuse burning towards a detonation. She looked away, gripping her glass, but she knew he was still gazing at her.

Unable to stand it any longer, Davina said a quick, 'Excuse me,' and hurried across the room to the door, putting her glass down on a table as she went. But once outside, she became afraid that Max might follow her, so she went over to

Reception to get her key and then went straight up
to her room. When she reached it she immediately
bolted the door, then told herself off for being a
fool; he was hardly likely to follow her here, and
she had left a perfectly good party just because a
man had been there who had once kissed her
against her will. For a few minutes she considered
going back, but she knew she wouldn't enjoy it
while Max was there. His frown of disapproval
would destroy any enjoyment and she would never
be able to relax with him in the room. Which was
silly and stupid and ridiculous! She shouldn't let
him get under her skin. He was just a bad-
tempered, sadistic . . .

Her thoughts broke off as she threw herself
frustratedly on to the bed, hitting at the pillows
with her fists. Why did he have to spoil
everything? Why? She wondered what he had been
about to say to her, but after only the briefest
conjecture rejected the idea that he might have
been going to apologise. Max wasn't the sort of
man to go around apologising for what he did.

Moodily Davina got up and went into the
bathroom to cream off her make-up, but she
didn't feel like going to bed, so she sat in a chair
and picked up the novel she'd started on the coach
that morning. She read it for the next hour or so,
her mind continuously wandering and having to be
brought firmly back to the book, trying to make
herself tired enough to sleep.

It was one of the times when she was
concentrating on the novel when the phone rang,
making her jump. She answered it to hear Giles's
voice. 'You frightened the life out of me!' she
complained. 'Do you know what time it is?'

'I'm sorry.' Giles's voice sounded urgent. 'Davina, I need your help. I slipped on the stairs and I've pulled a muscle. If Mike finds out he'll kill me. You know I stand a chance of getting in the England team.'

'Yes, all right.' Then, suspiciously, 'Are you sure this isn't some kind of joke? Because if it is . . .'

'No, really,' Giles answered earnestly. 'Please come and do something for my leg, Davina. It's room 322.'

Davina sighed and yawned. Funny how she hadn't felt tired until now, although it was one in the morning. At this time of the night there would be few people about, so she didn't bother to change or to put make-up on, just collected her equipment bag and went along to Giles's room. He had pulled the muscle, but it was nowhere near as bad as he feared. Davina put an ice-pack on it and then her portable heat lamp, finishing off with a stretch bandage. 'There, that should do for tonight. I'll leave my bag here and work on it again in the morning. And put a pillow under it tonight so that it's higher than your head, okay?'

'Okay. Thanks, Davina—I'm grateful. If Mike finds out . . .'

Tactfully refraining from asking him how he'd done it, although she strongly suspected he had been horsing around with some of the other men, Davina said flippantly, 'It will cost you a bunch of red roses at Christmas. Well, I'm going to bed. See you at eight tomorrow.'

She let herself out of his room and raised a weary hand to push her hair back from her face. Lord, she was tired! It would be good to get to . . . Her thoughts came to an abrupt stop as she saw

two men get out of the lift. They said good night to
each other, one turning in the opposite direction,
but the other coming towards her. And he, too,
stopped short when he saw her. 'Davina?' Max
began, then stiffened as he saw what room she'd
come out of. 'That's Giles Allinson's room!' he
exclaimed.

'Yes, but . . .' Davina bit her lip, not wanting to
give Giles away.

Max's face whitened. 'Come with me,' he
ordered, and led the way to a room only a short
way down the corridor from Giles's. He unlocked
the door and stood aside for her to enter.

'But this is—this is your room,' Davina
demurred as she hesitated in the doorway.

Max laughed harshly. 'You've just come out of
one man's room and you're quibbling about going
into another's?' Catching hold of her wrist, he
pulled her inside and shut the door with a slam. 'I
don't suppose I need ask what the hell you were
doing in there. It was perfectly obvious to anyone
who happened to be passing.'

'You've got it wrong,' she protested. 'And
anyway . . .'

'Oh, sure. That's what you say every time. You
plead the innocent and you look so—so unspoilt
that I was stupid enough to give you the benefit of
the doubt. But not this time. This time there can
be no doubt at all about what kind of woman you
are!'

'Oh. And just what kind of woman is that?'
Davina demanded, her temper rising.

'A gold-digger,' he told her bluntly. 'A girl
who's on the make and out to milk all she can out
of the situation. And you've really managed to get

yourself into a position where you can meet men with money; young, gullible men who will fall for your *obvious* attractions.'

He said the word 'obvious' with a contemptuous sneer, then added further insult by saying, 'I always wondered how you managed to get Bill Buckley to recommend you so highly. Did you go to bed with him, too? Is that how you did it?'

Davina took a furious step towards him, her right arm raised to hit him across the face. But Max's hand shot up and caught her wrist before the blow could land. 'You swine!' she yelled. 'Let go of me!' She tried to break free, then, when she couldn't, to hit out at him with her other hand, but he caught that too. 'You pig!' she shouted at him. 'Just who the hell do you think you are to talk to me like that?' She brought her leg up to try and kick his ankle, but Max held her at arm's length and then quickly jerked her forward so that she almost lost her balance and fell against him. She swore at him again, panting in her efforts to get free, more angry than she had ever been in her life. 'You rotten swine! Let go, I tell you!' But he held her wrists so tightly that her struggles were completely useless and she stopped, chest heaving, staring up at him with hatred in her hazel eyes. 'Or is it that you want to kiss me yourself?' she jeered breathlessly. 'Is that what this is all about? Well, go on, I can't stop you. If that's how you get your kicks. To force a girl into . . .'

'Stop it!' His exclamation broke through her anger and Davina stumbled as he pushed her violently away. 'You dangerous little cat! I'm not going to let you stay and breed trouble any longer. You're finished at the Club. I don't want you showing your face at the Rovers' ground ever again!'

'You can't do that,' Davina retaliated. 'You're not God Almighty. I've been taken on to the permanent staff and I can't be thrown out just on your say-so.'

Max's lips curled dangerously. 'You think not? You seem to forget that I brought a great deal of financial backing into the Club. And money talks.'

'You can't just condemn me out of hand. I've a right to be heard.'

'All right. Just what were you doing in Giles Allinson's room at two o'clock in the morning? Playing chess?' he said sarcastically.

Davina glared at him, her eyes on fire with anger. 'Mind your own damn business. You don't even merit an explanation!' she shot at him, then turned on her heel and marched out of the room, refusing to give him the satisfaction of hearing her plead, or of betraying Giles's confidence.

The next morning Davina was knocking on Giles's door on the stroke of eight, on time for the simple reason that she hadn't been able to sleep all night, even though she had been so physically tired. She had to hammer on the door quite loudly before Giles came to open it, yawning hugely and with his hand to his head.

'What's the time?' he mumbled.

'Eight o'clock. How's the leg?' Davina asked briskly as she walked in.

'Not too bad at all. My head aches, though.'

'Probably a hangover. Come on, let me look at your leg. I want my breakfast.'

She gave him half an hour of treatment, after which he hardly limped, then collected her bag and left him to get himself up. But instead of going in to breakfast, Davina left her things in Reception and then went for a walk. It was a fine, crisp morning, but as it was Sunday the city streets were mostly deserted. From somewhere the bells of a church began to ring and Davina walked towards the sound, coming eventually to an area of park-like garden round a big church. There was a wooden bench under a tree, its branches leafless now, and she sat under it, her hands in her pockets to keep them warm. The peace and quiet helped her to resolve a problem that she had been tossing and turning over all night. The problem of course was Max. It would have been easy to counter his accusations by telling him the truth, but that would have meant betraying Giles and there was no way she was going to do that, so she was faced with trying to brazen it out and staying on with a cloud of scandal over her head.

But there was another alternative. Davina looked up at the winter sun shining through the patterned branches of the tree and closed her eyes against the brightness. Whenever she and Max met the sparks flew; neither of them seemed to be able to help it, it was just some kind of chemical reaction like two elements warring with each other. In other people they might have fused and blended into one, but she and Max were like magnets that both attracted and repelled. She thought that Max wanted her, but his mind rebelled and kept his bodily needs in check, all except that one time when he had lost control and kissed her. And now he hated her because of it. As for herself . . . Davina hastily put that thought out of her mind, unwilling to try to analyse her own feelings. All that mattered was whether or not she could go on working at the Club in the kind of situation that Max had created. It was a good job and she didn't want to lose it, but last night had been more than she could take. She couldn't stand an atmosphere in which he might turn on her again at any moment, even if she did manage to stay on this time.

She rose from the bench, her decision made. On Monday she would go to the Club Secretary and tell him she wanted to leave. It would be a bitter thing to have to do because it probably meant they would never employ a woman physio again, but it was the only way she would get any peace of mind. It would be a victory, too, for Max, but he was welcome to that. Instinct told her she must get as far away from him as she could and as quickly as possible. To start her life over again and forget these last few months.

The coach had arrived when Davina got back to the hotel and she was one of the first to board it, sitting at the back with her bags on the seat beside her and opening a paper she had bought, the large pages hiding her face from the others. Giles got on among a bunch of the other players, who were probably helping to cover up for him, and Max came out a few minutes later with Mike Douglas and the rest of the Directors who had come to the match.

The men respected her obvious wish to be alone and settled down for the long journey home, watching a couple of films on the video screen or talking among themselves. Once Max got up to get himself a drink from the fridge near her seat and their glances met, but Davina looked quickly away and stared out of the window until he'd gone, her lips tightly together and a bitter look in her hazel eyes.

The players had been given Monday off, but Davina went into the Club in the morning to see the Club Secretary, but was daunted to find that he hadn't come in either.

'Is there anything I can do?' his secretary offered.

'No, it's all right. I suppose it can wait till tomorrow.'

Going down to the therapy room, Davina began to make a list of supplies she needed to replace. It was surprising how much bandage and creams she'd got through since she'd been there. For a moment she felt a touch of sadness, knowing that she wouldn't be there much longer, then she pulled herself together; she must ask the electrician to replace a fluorescent tube that was flickering and one of the wheels was a bit loose on the wheelchair that Max had supplied after their first big confrontation. But she mustn't think of Max or she would get angry again.

For the rest of the morning Davina worked in the therapy room, bringing her files up to date, wiping down the couch and her equipment with a mild disinfectant and generally bringing the room back to the high standard of cleanliness that she always tried to maintain. It was almost twelve and she was thinking about packing up for lunch when there was a brief rap on the door and Max walked in.

Davina's face paled and she moved behind the treatment couch as if it might give her some protection from the abrasive verbal assault she expected from him.

He hesitated for a moment in the doorway, then came in and shut the door. 'They told me in the main office that you wanted to see the Secretary. Is it something I can deal with?'

Her face set, Davina said shortly, 'I suppose you'd do just as well.' Going over to the desk, she opened her handbag and took out a sealed envelope. 'I wanted to give him this.' And she handed it to him.

Max glanced down at the Secretary's name on the front. 'Shall I open it?'

'By all means,' she agreed bitterly, and turned away, not wanting to see the triumph in his face.

She heard him tear the letter open and then there was a long silence, much longer than he would have needed to read it, for it was very short. But perhaps he was taking his time to gloat over her surrender. Tears pricked her eyes, but she blinked them back, then turned quickly as she heard a tearing sound. She stood amazed as Max tore the letter into shreds. 'Why?' She stared at him in utter disbelief.

'I talked to Giles this morning,' he said abruptly. 'He told me why you'd gone to his room.'

Davina frowned, trying to take it in, then she said slowly, 'Why did you speak to him about it?'

Somehow she couldn't see Max also tearing Giles off a strip for letting her visit him in his room, and this was confirmed when he hesitated, then admitted, 'I wanted to warn him against you. But as soon as he knew what I—suspected he told me that you'd gone there to treat his leg.'

'But surely you didn't believe him?' Davina said in bitter contemptuous mockery. 'Not when you're always so ready to think the worst of me.'

Max's mouth tightened. 'I suppose I deserve that.' His eyes took in her stormy face. 'I'm sorry, I was wrong,' he said brusquely.

Davina waited for him to go on, but instead he gave a brief nod and turned to leave. Furious, she ran forward and caught his sleeve, pulling him round so that he faced her. 'And that's it, is it? Just a simple "I'm sorry" is supposed to put everything right. Well, it doesn't. It isn't enough. You've accused me of incompetence, of being a gold-digger, and even—even of immorality. And an apology just isn't enough.'

'What do you want me to do—grovel at your feet for forgiveness?' demanded Max, becoming angry in his turn.

'Yes!' She yelled the word at him in a rage, her body trembling. 'Yes, why the hell not?'

He stiffened, his face frozen into a set mask. Davina saw that his hands were clenched into tight fists, the knuckles showing white, and suddenly realised she was on terribly dangerous ground. Her eyes flew to his face for a moment and then she turned away. 'Would you please wait?' she said shortly, and ran over to the desk, agitatedly pulling a piece of paper towards her. 'I want to give you this.'

'What is it?'

'My—my resignation.'

He stepped quickly over to her. 'I've already torn it up.'

'But I still want to leave. I can't—I can't work with you always—always breathing down my neck. I . . .' She broke off, her voice too agitated to go on.

Max leant forward and put a hand over hers,

stopping her from writing. The pen in her hand shook violently and his fingers tightened as he swore softly under his breath. *'I'm, sorry,'* he said again, but much more forcefully this time. 'I mean it. You don't have to leave.'

Davina shook her head. 'It's better that I go. I can't stay here knowing that you—that you . . .'

'That I what?' His tone was half challenging, yet strangely eager, as if he wanted her to identify what was between them, to bring it out into the open.

For a moment she was tempted to do so, to say, 'knowing that you want me', but her mind shied away from such a dangerously emotive declaration and she said instead, 'Knowing that you're likely to bawl me out for the slightest thing I do wrong. Just because you dislike me so much.'

'I don't—dislike you,' Max said curtly.

He was standing very close to her, his chest touching her back and shoulder as he leant across, still gripping her hand. Close enough for her to smell the masculine scents of soap and aftershave and to be aware of his strength and size. Close enough for her to easily turn and lift her face to be kissed. Or rejected. That thought made her ignore his words and say, 'I couldn't stay unless you promised to leave me alone to get on with my job. To—to stay away from me.'

Max withdrew his hand and stepped back. 'If that's what you wish.'

She turned to face him. 'Yes, it is,' she agreed clearly, trying desperately to keep her emotions hidden under a façade of coolness and determination. 'I—I won't stay unless you do.'

'Then you have my word,' he answered coldly. 'I

won't—bother you again.' He turned and walked to the door, but paused before he opened it. 'For what it's worth, I think you're a very good physio.' His mouth twisted wryly. 'The Club are lucky to have your services.' And he turned and left.

As soon as he'd gone, Davina sank into a chair, her whole body shaking uncontrollably. So she was staying, and Max had promised to keep away from her. It should have been an enormous relief and made her happy, but somehow all she could think of was Max saying that he didn't dislike her and what would have happened if she'd taken the other course, if she had turned to him instead of keeping still. Such a small difference, but one that she instinctively knew had been a very great decision. Had she been a coward or had it been good common sense? She closed her eyes and saw his face again; remembering his thinly handsome features, the straight, unyielding mouth and his grey eyes that were sometimes pale as winter ice and sometimes stormy-dark with need. Davina trembled convulsively. She'd taken the right course, the only one. Max was a man whose icy coldness hid scarcely suppressed fires beneath the surface, fires that threatened to erupt whenever she was near to innocently create the spark which melted his veneer of ice. He was dangerous and she was afraid of him, but whether she was more afraid when he hated her or when he wanted her, she didn't know.

Max kept his word and stayed away from her; she hardly saw him for about three weeks and then only at a distance. And during those three weeks Davina came to a couple of momentous decisions. The first was to tell Peter that she was sorry but she didn't want to go out with him any more. He was upset, of course, and wanted to know if she had met someone else. Davina denied it and could only repeat that she was sorry.

'But why?' he protested. 'I don't understand.'

'Nor do I, really,' she admitted unhappily. 'I just don't want to be tied to anyone.'

'But you're not tied to me. Is that what you're trying to say—that you want us to get engaged or something?'

'*No*! That's the last thing . . .' She shook her head. 'I'm sorry, I didn't mean it like that. I just want to be free for a while.'

Peter nodded. 'All right, but you know I'll be around if you change your mind or get lonely.' He shrugged. 'It's a shame, though. Especially with Christmas coming up.'

So she escaped from that casual relationship quite lightly and was glad she had, realising now that it was the kind in which two people could get so used to each other that they just drifted into marriage and possibly even into love in time.

To compensate, Davina took her second decision, to buy herself a car. She consulted Bill Buckley and he helped her to choose a nippy little blue hatchback which was economical on petrol and a good bargain. It was stretching her resources a bit to pay for that and the flat, but Davina told herself she deserved a Christmas present; sometimes it did you good to be a bit impetuous and treat yourself to something you really wanted.

The Friday before Christmas was a big day in the Rovers' calendar. It was the day the Club gave a party for the children of all the employees,

players and ground staff alike. Everyone, including
Davina, had been roped in to help, and she spent
the entire morning wrapping parcels and tying
name tags on them with Mike Douglas's wife and
one of the typists. She was also to serve the food,
so she went home for a quick lunch and to change
into a pale blue jump-suit with a gay scarf tied at
her neck. The children started arriving at two-
thirty, party-clean and pretty, excited anticipation
in their eyes. Davina helped take them over from
their mums or dads and the little ones off with
their coats and gloves. They had some games first
in the gym to warm them up, and afterwards a
Punch and Judy show which they all loved,
whatever their age. Then they were let loose in the
room where the food had been set out on two rows
of tables. And let loose was the operative
expression; they ran in with loud whoops of
delight, the boys leading the way, and charged into
the food as if they hadn't eaten for a week.

Calls for more lemonade or orange juice kept
Davina running up and down the tables until they
could eat no more and the little ones had begun to
get over-excited and cry. She wiped them down
and got several sticky fingermarks on her jump-
suit in the process and made them cheerful again
with whispered promises of Father Christmas.
That immediately cheered them up again, and they
all went back to the gym where they found the red-
coated Santa sitting beneath the lit Christmas tree,
sacks of parcels all round him. There were oohs and
aahs and the children crowded forward, the tiny
ones a little shyly.

'Hallo there, children. Merry Christmas!' Santa
boomed out, and Davina looked up, startled, and

trying to see behind the frothy white whiskers. She had known that someone from the Club was to dress up as Father Christmas, but she had never imagined it would be Max!

With much ho-ho-hoing, he began to call out the children's names as he took the toys from the sacks, and mostly they went rushing up, but he called out one name and it was some time before they could find the child because she was too shy to go up to him. Davina took the little girl's hand and coaxed her nearer, but she hung back, on the point of bursting into tears.

'Hallo, Carol,' Max said gently. 'Don't be afraid. Why don't you come and see my funny old beard? It tickles, you know.' And he blew at his whiskers, making them lift in the air. The little girl slowly relaxed her hold on Davina's hand and moved nearer until Max could lift her on to his knee. He was wonderfully gentle with the child, talking to her and playing with her until she had conquered her fear and was laughing with him, then he gave her her present and she ran happily away. He was the same with the other shy children, refusing to be hurried and putting them at ease before giving them their presents. Davina had moved to the side of the room and stood watching, seeing a completely different side of Max, one that she had never expected. He was so tender and kind. She wondered if he had ever wanted children of his own, whether that fatal car crash had killed those hopes too.

A lump came to her throat and her eyes pricked, but she bit her lip hard. So maybe Max was human after all. So what? Whatever kind of hell he was going through was his own—he'd made that more than clear. She couldn't do anything about it and didn't want to. He would just have to sort out his own problems.

The party came to an end and Davina was kept busy finding the children's coats, sorting out a few squabbles—and then there were the leftovers to clear up. It took a good couple of hours, and at seven there was just herself and a typist left. The other girl looked anxiously at her watch. 'Do you mind if I go, Davy? I've got a date tonight.'

'No, that's okay. I'll finish off. There's not much to do now.'

'Oh, thanks.' The typist grabbed her coat and then gave an exclamation. 'The Santa suit! I promised to take it back to the shop tonight; they want it for another party tomorrow.'

'But it will be shut now, won't it?'

'No, they're staying open late tonight because there are so many parties going on tomorrow. Oh, darn, that means I'll be late anyway.'

'It's all right, I'll take it. Where is it?'

'Down in the changing room. Thanks, Davy, I really appreciate it. Here's the receipt. And there's a ten-pound deposit to collect.'

She rushed off, leaving Davina to take the last bags of rubbish downstairs to the dustbins. Then she put on her jacket and went down to the changing rooms. The suit was there, hanging on a hanger, and looking incongruously forlorn without all the padding. The beard and wig were in a plastic bag on a bench. Davina stepped to pick it up and as she did so her foot kicked something that had fallen under the bench. Stooping, she felt under the bench and brought it out. It was a man's wallet, evidently dropped when someone had been

changing. The Rovers had a big lost property
department for all the things left behind by the
fans, but it wouldn't be open now, and anyway
this obviously belonged to someone from the
Club. She went up to the office to hand it in there,
but everyone had gone, she seemed to be the only
person left in the place. Frowning, Davina decided
to look inside the wallet, knowing it was Friday
and whoever it belonged to wouldn't get it back
until Monday, which could be extremely inconvenient, especially if he was going out to
celebrate or do Christmas shopping over the
weekend.

It was a thick wallet and contained a small wad
of fifty-pound notes as well as a whole profusion
of credit cards. Davina pulled one out and saw
that the wallet belonged to Max. He must have
dropped it when he was changing into the Santa
Claus costume. She had already half decided to
take the wallet to its owner, but now she hesitated,
wondering what to do. But Max, just like any
other man, would need his money this weekend
and it would be unfair of her not to return it just
because it was his. And anyway, he would be
wondering where on earth it was. All she need do
was to hand him the wallet and then leave. Her
mind reluctantly made up, Davina found his
address, which was a village some fifteen miles or
so from Redford, and ran down to her car.

'You the last?' the doorman asked rather
wearily. 'I can lock up, then. Been a long day, it
has today,' he grumbled.

'Sorry.' But why she should feel obliged to
apologise when it wasn't her fault, Davina didn't
know.

After dropping off the Santa costume, she consulted her map and drove out to Max's village. She had been there a couple of times before, though not for several years, but she remembered it as a pretty place with old, wooden-beamed cottages and a couple of pubs clustering round a stone church and a village green. It was probably a conservation area now and wildly expensive to live in. It was already very dark and rather misty, the street lights dim as she drove along. When she got to the village green, Davina had to stop and go into the pub to ask the way to Max's house. The landlord directed her down an unlit lane, past a couple of thatched cottages to a farmyard-type gate with the name Quenbury carved into it. She got out of the car to open the gate, leaving it open on its hook because she wouldn't be there more than two minutes.

The air felt damp and very cold. She shivered and wished she'd remembered to shut the car door, now all the warmth had gone. The driveway was long and tree-lined, ending in a gravel circle before a large Tudor house. Wow! Even in the darkness she could see that it was long and sprawling. There was a bright light on by the front door and she could see a light in a room farther along, but mostly the curtains were drawn to shut out the unpleasant weather. Switching off the engine, Davina got out of the car and walked over to the front door, her footsteps crunching on the soft gravel. There was an old bell-pull at the side of the door and she heard a bell ringing inside as she pulled it down. From somewhere inside she heard a dog barking and then the noise died as if the animal had been shut into a room. She heard footsteps coming towards the door and her heart began to beat painfully in her chest, her pulses to race.

Max opened the door and stiffened in surprise. 'Davina!' he exclaimed.

'H-hallo, Max.' She found she was trembling, and said in a rush, 'I found your wallet at the Club. You must have dropped it while you were changing. I thought you might have missed it by now, so I brought it over for you.' And she held the wallet out to him.

'Thank you.' He took it from her. 'You're shaking!'

'It—it's cold.'

'Then you must come in and have a drink to warm you up.'

'Oh, no. I have to get back.'

'It won't take a minute to make a coffee. And I haven't thanked you for coming so far out of your way. Please come in.' He put a firm hand under her elbow and drew her inside. 'Don't you have any gloves? You're freezing,' he commented as he shut the door behind her.

Davina found herself in a large stone-flagged hallway with a beautifully carved staircase going to the upper floor.

'No, really. I have to get back to Redford,' she said nervously, hanging back, and realising that she shouldn't be here, that she should just have turned and gone.

But Max was leading her into a lovely sitting room with a beamed ceiling and a huge inglenook fireplace where a log about three feet long burned on the iron grate, its heat warming the room, its flames drawing her towards their brightness.

'That's right—you stand there and get warm while I make the coffee. I won't be more than a minute.' At the door he turned to look back at her and gave a small smile. 'Don't run away,' he said softly.

He must have been psychic, the thought had already crossed her mind to leave as soon as his back was turned, even though she realised that such an action now would be childish and cowardly. And she was a grown woman, she ought to be able to handle this kind of situation. The situation, yes, she answered herself, but not Max. She had no idea how to handle Max.

The room was warm and cosy with its thick velvet curtains, beautiful Chinese carpet on the stone floor and large, comfortable Chesterfield settees. There were pictures on the walls, portraits and watercolours, and several pieces of good antique furniture, some of the small tables with photographs in silver frames on them. Was one of them, she wondered, of his wife? She moved nearer to one of the tables, bending to look at the photographs. There were some of Max with other people, but none of him alone with a woman and no wedding photograph, and there were two of women by themselves, but they were dressed in an old-fashioned way and Davina guessed they would be older now, too old to be Max's wife. She heard him coming back and stepped quickly away from the table again.

He set the coffee tray down and began to pour. 'How do you take your coffee?'

'White, please, but no sugar.'

He handed the cup to her, his eyes for a moment searching her face. 'I hear you bought yourself a

car,' he remarked, turning to pour his own cup.
'What make is it?'

Relieved to be on a safe subject, Davina told
him all about it, but stopped when she realised she
was nervously talking too much.

But Max merely said, 'Yes, I think you've made
a good choice. Shall we sit down?' And he crossed
to one of the settees.

'I can't stay.'

'Of course not. But it seems a little odd to stand.
How have you got the car insured?'

Davina sat down on the edge of the settee
opposite to him. 'Fully comprehensive. I thought
that was best.'

'Much the wisest thing,' he agreed.

A silence fell between them that Davina couldn't
stand. 'I—I thought I heard a dog barking,' she
blurted.

'Mm, that's Buster. He's a Great Dane.'

'Buster? You called a Great Dane Buster?'

Max's mouth twisted in amusement. 'Don't you
like it?'

'It doesn't seem very apt somehow.'

'Perhaps not. People generally get a surprise
when they see him.'

He didn't continue, and to avoid a silence
Davina said quickly, 'This is a lovely house.'

'Thank you. Would you like to see round it?'

'Oh, no! I didn't mean . . .'

'I know you didn't, but you might as well look
round while you're here, if you'd like to.'

Davina tried hard, but curiosity won, so he took
her on a conducted tour through the house. It was
different from what she had expected; all the
rooms were heated—to keep out the damp, Max

said—but most of them had the furniture covered in dust sheets because he didn't normally use them, so there was an air of desolation about those rooms. He only used the wing of the house nearest the front door which contained, downstairs, the sitting room, a study and a large kitchen with a utility room opening off it where she was introduced to the dog, a beautiful blue-grey coloured animal that stood nearly three feet tall. And upstairs there were two bedrooms, one of them with a bathroom en suite. Davina marvelled at what she saw, but was left with an impression of deep loneliness. Is this what happens to a man when he loses his wife? she wondered. Does he lose all interest in the way he lives? The house was beautiful, it was a shame to shut most of it up. She wondered why he didn't sell it and buy something smaller.

'Has the house always been in your family?' she asked.

'Only about a hundred years or so.'

Only about a hundred years! But perhaps that wasn't long in the history of a house that had stood since the sixteenth century.

When they got back to the hall Davina said with formal politeness, 'Thank you for the coffee and the tour. I have to go now.'

'Of course. Thank you again for bringing the wallet. I'm very grateful. It was a good party for the children, wasn't it?'

'Oh yes, it was,' Davina agreed warmly. She remembered how gentle he had been. So different. And different now, too. He seemed at ease in his own home, with no anger in his face, and it helped her to relax a little. But the need hadn't gone, she was still aware of that, although he had it under iron control except for a moment at the door when he said tautly, 'Must you go?'

It could have been taken as the polite question of a host, simply a matter of good manners, and Davina chose to take it that way. 'I'm afraid so. Good night.'

'Good night, Davina.' Max reached past her to open the door and they were met with a thick, choking fog that lay heavily in the glow of the porchlight. 'Good grief!' Max exclaimed. 'You surely didn't drive through that? But no, it was quite clear when you came, wasn't it?'

'It had started to get misty,' Davina admitted. 'But nowhere near as bad as this.' She pulled her jacket closer together and moved to step into it.

'You can't go in this. It's much too thick,' protested Max.

'But I must.'

'Nonsense. You won't even get safely down the driveway.'

'But I must go home. What else can I do?' she exclaimed agitatedly.

For a moment he was silent, then he said tightly, 'You'll just have to stay here for the night.'

CHAPTER SIX

DAVINA stiffened and for a moment stood very still. Max, too, was silent, waiting, the tension between them as real and yet as ephemeral as the fog. She looked out into the night again, wondering whether she could possibly make it, but knew that he was right and she would either run off the road or have to spend the night in the car. 'Perhaps—perhaps it will clear later,' she said rather desperately.

'Possibly. But I wouldn't bank on it; it looks as if it's set in for the night.'

Davina stepped back so that he could close the big oak door, feeling as if her escape was being cut off and she was Max's prisoner. She lifted her head to look at him uncertainly, searching his face for some intimation of what he was thinking, but it gave nothing away beyond a certain tautness round his mouth.

They went back into the sitting room and sat down again. Max made another coffee and for a while he talked about the history of the house, but he spoke almost automatically and Davina wasn't really listening. After half an hour she got up to look out of the window, but if anything the fog was even denser. Neither of them said anything, but their thoughts were full of the long night ahead, alone under the same roof. At one point Max went out into the kitchen to feed Buster, and Davina ran to the window to look out again. The fog seemed to curl about the house like a living thing, holding it close in its embrace, trying to get in. Davina shivered, feeling suddenly cold despite the warmth of the fire and the central heating.

'I'm afraid there's no help for it.' Max's dry voice came from behind her. 'You'll have to stay.'

Davina let the curtain fall into place and slowly turned to face him. 'Yes, I'm afraid you're right.'

'Is there anyone you'd like to phone to tell them?'

She shook her head. 'No. I live alone.'

For a second their eyes met, but then Max looked almost hurriedly away. 'Are you hungry? How about some supper?'

Davina's mind wasn't exactly on food and she didn't feel particularly hungry, having had a few sandwiches at the party, but getting supper sounded like a safe way to use up some of the time, so she nodded and said, 'Yes, I am rather. If it isn't too much trouble.'

'None at all. Why don't you come and give me a hand?'

They went into the kitchen and Davina cut bread and butter while Max baked potatoes in the microwave and topped them with ham and cheese. He worked efficiently, evidently used to caring for himself, and the kitchen was spotlessly clean.

'Shall we eat at the table in here, or would you prefer to take trays into the sitting room?' asked Max when the food was ready.

'In the sitting room, I think,' Davina decided, not wanting to have the intimacy of sitting across a table from him.

There was a TV set in the room which Max turned on and they watched a wild life documentary while they ate, but Davina was unable to concentrate on it even though she kept her eyes on the screen or on her plate, carefully never looking in Max's direction. But there wasn't a second when she wasn't intensely aware of him, and she sensed that he felt the same. She ate some of her supper but soon found that she was far too tense to eat, that she could hardly swallow. After a while she gave up even pretending to try and put the tray on the floor.

Max glanced across. 'Had enough?'

'Yes, thank you. I—I wasn't so hungry after all.'

It seemed that he wasn't either, because he almost immediately stood up and carried the trays into the kitchen.

Those few minutes that he was away were the longest in Davina's life. She flew to the window again in the vain hope that the fog had lifted, but it was just as thick. Then she went to stand in front of the fire, defensively facing the door, her heart beating too fast and her nerves taut as stretched elastic. Max came back into the room and closed the door, then stood still as he saw her facing him so apprehensively. He looked at her for a moment, his eyes narrowing, then he walked slowly towards her.

With the fire behind her, Davina couldn't back away, she could only stand there, gazing into his face as he came to stand only a few explosive inches away. It seemed that all pretence at normality was over. His eyes devoured her as she stood in the firelight, the glow from the flames turning her hair into a golden halo around her head, her eyes wide and lips slightly parted in trepidation. The tension between them had been there all evening, but now it was out in the open, accentuated by recognition.

Max's eyes grew dark as he slid them slowly over her, coming back to her face. 'I kissed you once,' he said harshly, as if the words were torn out of him. 'I want to kiss you again.'

Davina stood perfectly still, gazing into his eyes, completely unable to speak.

His jaw tightened and his hands clenched. 'But I won't,' he said shortly. 'You don't have to be afraid. I won't try anything. Even though I wa . . .' He broke off, biting his lip, but it was obvious that he had been going to say, even though I want you. For a long moment he gazed into her eyes, waiting for her to speak, to admit that she wanted him too, but when she continued to look at him in silence, he turned abruptly away. 'If you'll come with me I'll find you some night clothes.'

Numbly Davina followed him up the wide oak staircase and waited while he went into his bedroom and came out with a pair of blue silk pyjamas and a dressing-gown. 'I'm afraid these will be rather large for you, but they're all I have. If you'd like to use the bathroom now I'll make up the other bed. Oh, you'll find a new toothbrush in the bathroom cabinet.'

'Thank you.' Davina took the things from him, her hands trembling.

Max shot her a quick look. 'I told you, you don't have to be afraid of me. Unless,' his voice sharpened, 'unless it isn't fear.'

Her eyes hunted, Davina looked away. 'I don't—I don't know,' she admitted on a strangled note, then turned and ran into the bathroom, bolting the door firmly behind her.

After a few minutes she stripped off her clothes and began to wash, cursing herself for having made such a stupid admission. But it was true, she just didn't know how she felt. As she looked at herself in the mirror as she washed off her make-up, Davina's hand slowly stilled. She might not know how she felt about Max, but she did know that she wanted him sexually. Almost as much as he wanted her. This electricity that charged between them, this tension, and the feverish agitation she felt were proof enough of that, even though she had refused to face it until now. And even though she'd fought him when he kissed her, it had set her on fire with a need that she hadn't known existed before. So why not tell him and enjoy what they both wanted?

But it wasn't as simple as that. Nothing ever was. If she gave herself to him, would it be just for that one night and then, their needs fulfilled, would it be over? Just a sordid little one-night stand. Or would Max want it to go on? Would they become lovers? She be his mistress? The very word sounded distasteful and she flinched away from it. But she had no illusions about Max wanting to marry her. He had made it more than plain that he resented the desire she aroused in him. So she knew that was out. But it seemed that at least the choice was to be hers. Davina brushed her hair, then put on Max's pyjamas. They were much too big for her and she had to turn them up at the ankles and wrists, and his dressing-gown swamped her. She went out on to the landing and found Max waiting for her.

He straightened up, his body rigid, unable to hide the fierce blaze of need in his eyes. Then,

'Dear God, you look so young!' he exclaimed as he took in her bare feet and unmade-up face. 'Like a child.'

She wanted to tell him that she wasn't a child, that she was woman enough to be taken to his bed, but she was so nervous, her throat so dry, that the words wouldn't come. And then the moment was gone. Max said, 'Good night, Davina,' in a grim, hopeless kind of voice and strode quickly into his own room, shutting the door firmly behind him.

Davina hardly slept at all that night. She crept into the cool sheets and lay listening to Max moving around in the room next door. She couldn't hear very well even though her senses were stretched and alert, but he seemed to be pacing, then his door opened and she heard him go quickly down the stairs. She waited for him to come back, knowing that there was no lock on her door and he only had to walk in. But there was no sound for a long time except for a church clock somewhere nearby that rang out the hours; midnight, two, four. At last Davina fell into an uneasy sleep that was near to wakefulness, stirring at every strange sound but too exhausted to wake completely.

Daylight filtering through the curtains woke her at six-thirty and she decided she must get up and leave at once, but she turned over and the next minute fell into a really deep sleep, not waking again until she heard a bell ringing loudly. For a moment she thought it was her alarm clock, but then the bell was followed by a loud knocking and she sat up, fully awake and aware that she was in Max's house. And it sounded as if there was someone at the door. Davina waited for Max to answer it, but the knocking came again. Reluctantly she got up and pulled on the dressing-gown, then went out on to the landing and called Max's name outside his door. 'Max, there's someone at the door!' He didn't answer and she knocked, then gingerly pushed wide his already partly open door. He wasn't in the room and his bed hadn't been slept in.

Agitatedly Davina ran down the stairs, thinking that whoever was at the door and ringing again must be something to do with Max. Fleeting nightmares of his having gone for a walk in the fog, of having an accident, went through her mind as she sped to open the front door, hampered by the over-long pyjamas. Her hands trembled in her haste, but at last she pulled it open.

'Morning,' the man at the door began. 'Thought you'd forgotten I was . . .' His words broke off as he blinked at Davina, his eyes going over her in astonishment.

Equally taken aback, Davina found herself staring at one of the groundsmen from the Club. After a stunned moment when her mind was too frozen to think, she hastily pulled the dressing-gown tightly around her and knotted the belt. 'Did—did you want Mr Blair?'

'That's right. He asked me to come and do a job for him whenever I had a morning free. So as the team aren't playing today I thought I'd come over. Still in bed, is he?' he asked with a definite leer.

Davina felt the blood rush to her face, but said as coolly as she could, 'I've no idea. I found his wallet at the Club last night and brought it over, but the fog was so thick I couldn't get home.'

'Fog?' The man laughed and glanced eloquently up at the clear sky. 'There wasn't any fog in Redford!' And he laughed again as if he thought it was a good joke.

Before Davina could insist, there was the sound of barking and Max came round the corner of the house with Buster on a lead. He took in the situation at a glance and frowned, coming quickly up to them. Davina just turned and fled back upstairs to dress.

When she came down, Max was in the kitchen alone. 'I've made you scrambled eggs on toast,' he told her. 'Is that all right?'

'Yes, fine, thank you.' And she sat down at the table.

'I'm sorry about that,' he said tautly. 'I'd forgotten that Saunders might come this morning.'

He set a mug of coffee in front of her and Davina put her hands round it, gazing into the dark, liquid depths. 'I told him about the fog, but he didn't believe me. He said there wasn't any in Redford.'

'Yes, I know. It must have been isolated in this area. We're not far from the river here.'

She looked up at him. 'He thinks—he thinks . . .'

'Yes, it's perfectly obvious what he thinks,' Max agreed grimly. 'There's nothing we can do about it.'

'But surely you told him, explained?'

'I merely told him you'd got stuck in the fog. If I'd made a big thing of it it would only have confirmed his suspicions.'

'But he'll tell everyone,' Davina protested.

Max shrugged. 'Yes, I expect he will. But if

we ignore the rumours they'll be forgotten in time.'

Davina stared at him, astonished that he could take it so calmly. 'But don't you care about your—your reputation?'

For a second he looked amused. 'Not really. But I care about yours,' he added, frowning. 'I'm sorry it's happened, but I honestly think the best thing to do is to ignore it.'

'All right,' Davina agreed reluctantly. She finished her eggs and stood up. 'I must go. Thank you for breakfast.'

He didn't try to detain her and she drove hurriedly away from the house as he watched her from the doorway, a lonely figure with only the dog for company.

The Rovers were due to play an away match in the north today, but it had been postponed because the opponents' ground was waterlogged, so Davina had her first Saturday free since August. She used it to do the last of her Christmas shopping and to wrap the gifts she had bought for her family and friends. She was spending Christmas with her ex-flatmate, her parents having decided to go away for the holiday, so on the Monday she drove down to Kent to see them and to give them their presents. They found her rather abstracted, her thoughts elsewhere, and often told her something and then had to repeat it because she hadn't been listening. She felt restless and frustrated, her mind going often back to Max and that moment on the landing when she just might have chosen differently if he hadn't made the choice for her.

The rumour that they were lovers had spread

like wildfire through the Club, just as she had
foreseen. She got knowing looks from some of the
men and curious ones from the girls in the general
office, but no one came right out and asked her.
Davina didn't know whether to be pleased about
this or not. At least if they'd asked her she could
have denied it. Perhaps it was lucky that it was
Christmas week; people had other things on their
minds and were busy, so she was able to keep to
herself. She knew that Max came to the Club to
attend the Directors' Christmas get-together, but
she made sure that she had to go and pick up some
supplies from the wholesalers while that was going
on and didn't see him.

Several invitations to go out to parties in that
week had been sent to her, but Davina just didn't
feel like going to them. Once she forced herself to
go, but she felt like an onlooker, a stranger, unable
to join in even though she had known most of the
people there nearly all her life. She came home
early but couldn't settle to do anything, her mind
on Max alone in that large house. The rest of the
parties she cancelled, pleading a cold, but she was
too restless to just sit at home and went out for
long walks round the shopping centre or through
the local park.

All the employees at the Club had a drinks party
on Christmas Eve afternoon, but Davina left early,
again pleading her imaginary cold. She had bought
herself a small silver Christmas tree and hung it
with a few baubles. It stood on the coffee table in
the sitting room and she sat in a chair looking at it
while the day darkened around her. Suddenly she
stood up and ran to change and pack a bag, then
made a hurried phone call to her ex-flatmate.

Quickly she checked the rest of the flat and ran to the door, but stopped and went back for the Christmas tree, carrying it in her hand as she ran down to the car.

The roads round Redford were busy with holiday traffic and Davina had to drive slowly but impatiently until she reached more open countryside, then she put her foot down, the miles flying by until she reached Max's house. There were no lights on and she hesitated, afraid he must have gone away, but the compulsion that had brought her there made her get out of the car and ring the bell, her bag at her feet and the silly Christmas tree in her hands.

From deep in the house the dog barked and her heart quickened; he would never have gone away and left the dog. The light above her head snapped on and then Max opened the door. He stared at her, his eyes widening.

All the way over Davina had been wondering what she could say, what words to use to tell him. But she didn't have to say anything. One look at her face and he knew. 'Oh, dear God!' he breathed, and put out a hand to touch her as if she might not be real. Then he pulled her roughly inside and the next moment she was in his arms, Christmas tree and all, and he was kissing her with a savage hunger.

'The tree,' she protested as soon as she could breathe, but he put his hands on either side of her face and kissed her again. 'Max, we ought to set it up.'

'What tree? Oh. Tomorrow.'

He let go of her long enough to pull her bag inside and shut the door, then took the tree from her and put it on the hall table. 'Tomorrow,' he said again, his eyes fixed on her face.

For a moment Davina felt shy, but she was given no time to indulge it as Max picked her up in his arms and carried her up the stairs, shouldering open the door of his room and taking her inside.

He held her, looking down into her face as if for reassurance, as if he still couldn't quite believe that this was happening. Then he gently set her down on her feet and kissed her again.

'I want you,' he murmured against her lips, his hands beginning to take off her clothes. 'I've wanted you from the moment I first saw you.' Her coat fell on the floor and his breathing quickened as his fingers moved to unbutton her sweater. 'I want to take you to my bed. But first I want to touch and kiss you. I want to take off your clothes and touch your skin, feel its softness.' He opened her sweater and saw that she wasn't wearing anything underneath, and his hands began to shake. 'Oh, dear sweet God! You're so beautiful— so perfect.'

Her sweater, too, fell to the floor and she stepped out of her shoes as Max took off her skirt and then went down on one knee to take off her tights. From that position he gazed up at her hungrily, his eyes avid for her youth and beauty, then he reached to take off her panties. Davina closed her eyes but could feel his scorching gaze as he explored her. Then she let out a gasping moan as he kissed her, his mouth working along her body, his hands, his lips touching, caressing, arousing her to a great heat of desire. She fumbled at his clothes, trying to pull them off, but too aroused by what he was doing to her to concentrate. He kissed her breasts, the nipples long since aroused, muttering words in his throat as he did so, words of endearment, of need and yearning. 'Oh, God, it's been so long!'

His hands, his voice, his body shook with desire as he passionately took her mouth again, and he feverishly began to help her to take off his clothes. She wanted to look at him and touch him, too, but there was no time. His overpowering need for her body dominated him as he bore her back on to the bed and came down on to her. 'It's been so long. So many years. Davina! Davina!' He groaned out her name as he began to make love to her, his body one with hers.

Davina clung to him, her fingers gripping his shoulders, both their bodies slippery with sweat as she moved against him, her moaning breath rising on a growing tide of pleasure. Max's body began to jerk in frenzied, uncontrollable excitement, his hands on her hips bruising her skin, and then their voices mingled in a groaning climax of shared ecstasy and fulfilment.

Max slumped down beside her and Davina could feel his heart thumping in his chest. His body trembled and a lock of hair had fallen down over his forehead, making him look somehow vulnerable. He slowly opened his eyes to look at her, then reached up a hand to pull her head nearer so that he could kiss her, his breath still ragged and uneven. They lay still then until their breathing became regular again. Lifting himself on to one elbow, Max gently began to push the hair from her damp forehead. His face seemed different; the tightness had gone from around his mouth, and there was a triumphant, almost peaceful look in his grey eyes. 'I'm sorry,' he said gently. 'I was probably too fast for you.'

'No.' Davina felt herself begin to blush. 'No, you weren't.'

'Good.' He smiled at her. 'I love the way you blush.'

'D-do you?'

'Mmm.' He bent to kiss her flushed cheeks, then her nose and her eyes. 'But I can do much better than that.' His fingers began to caress her quivering body. 'You'll enjoy it far more next time.'

'Next time?'

His eyes looked into hers, already darkening with desire again. 'This time,' he breathed, and began to make love to her for a second time.

When Davina woke the next morning she knew exactly where she was. Max still lay asleep beside her, one of his arms and a leg thrown possessively over hers. The clock on top of a chest of drawers said almost ten-thirty. Ten-thirty on Christmas Morning. And what a Christmas Eve! Davina smiled in contented remembrance, her finger-bruised body more than satiated. Max had said it had been years since he had made love to a woman, but he had certainly made up for a great part of it last night. She turned her head to study him, wishing there was more light. He seemed very relaxed, the sweep of his eyelashes caressing his cheeks, his mouth curved as if he was having a very pleasant dream. Davina blew gently on his face and he stirred, wrinkling his nose and then opening his eyes to look at her. 'Hi,' she said softly. 'Merry Christmas.'

He grinned. 'Merry Christmas.' And he pulled

her over so that she was half lying on him. 'Aren't you going to kiss me good morning?'

She did so, taking her time about it, exploring his mouth as there had been no time to do last night, probing, tasting his lips, until his hand went behind her head and they kissed in rising passion. Max relaxed his grip for a moment and she raised her head, lips parted sensuously, her breathing uneven. 'You know something?' he said thickly. 'I rather think I have a Christmas present for you.'

Davina's eyes widened. 'Max!' She began to laugh, but then gasped as he began to show her just what he meant.

That Christmas Day was the most wonderful that Davina had ever spent. They did everything together; setting up her little Christmas tree, cooking lunch, taking Buster for a long walk. They were very close physically, often stopping what they were doing as Max kissed her in possessive hunger, his appetite for her in no way satisfied, and they walked arm in arm, their bodies close. There was a wood near Max's house and they took the dog there, letting him run loose as they walked in the crisp winter morning sunshine. Once, after they had stopped to kiss, Max held her and said, 'What made you come to me last night?'

Slowly Davina shook her head. 'I don't really know. It was a sudden decision—and yet it wasn't.' She laughed a little. 'That sounds typically female, doesn't it? I'd been thinking about you all week, ever since I spent the night here. You were on my mind all the time and I felt so . . .' She hesitated, flushing.

'Tell me,' Max insisted.

'Well, I felt so sort of empty and restless.'

'I think frustrated is the word you're looking for.'

She smiled. 'Very likely.'

'And do you feel frustrated now?' he asked as he began to kiss her neck.

'No, but I may well begin to if you don't stop doing that.'

But he didn't stop, instead moulding her body against his, his hands inside her coat, until at length he raised his head and said huskily, 'There's a big log fire burning in the grate back at the house—and a thick fur rug in front of it,' he added suggestively.

Davina caught her breath and then nodded, so they turned, their footsteps quickening, and went back to make love throughout the afternoon, the flames casting shadows on their naked bodies entwined before the fire. Afterwards Max opened up the dining room, removing the dust sheets from the long refectory table so that they could eat in style. He got out old silver candelabra and they ate their Christmas dinner by candlelight, sitting close together, their knees, their hands often touching as they laughed and talked, and often fell silent as they gazed into each other's eyes, each thinking of the night that was to come. And it wasn't even ten o'clock before Max impatiently pulled her to her feet and headed for the stairs.

'The dishes . . .' Davina protested feebly.

'Don't be silly.'

He kissed her, and as they walked up the stairs she felt as if she was being transported into a future of excitement and passion.

CHAPTER SEVEN

DAVINA'S mental clock woke her at eight the next morning. She yawned and peered at the clock on the dresser to verify the time, then groaned inwardly, snuggling up to Max and wishing she didn't have to get up. He stirred and reached for her, but she laughed and said, 'Not this morning. I have to go to work, remember?'

'You can't possibly go today,' he stated firmly, and put his arm round her.

'But I must.' Davina ran her fingers lightly across his smooth chest. 'You know the Rovers are playing a Boxing Day charity match this afternoon and there's a practice this morning, so I have to be there.' She giggled. 'Otherwise I might get the sack. There's a certain Director who has a down on me,' she teased.

'If you go on doing that a certain Director will certainly come down on you,' Max retorted, capturing her hand and pulling her close to kiss her. 'Good morning,' he murmured. 'Thank you for another wonderful night.' He began to kiss her hand, burying his mouth in her palm. Davina loved it and moved sensuously against him, but then remembered the time and drew reluctantly away. Max groaned. 'I know, I know! Okay, let's go and shower.'

Davina sat up. 'Who goes first?'

Max, too, sat up and looked at her bare breasts. 'We both go together,' he decided very firmly.

So Davina was late getting to the Club anyway, although she wasn't the only one; everyone seemed to be reluctant to come to work today. Most of the players were extremely responsible men, knowing that their very good livelihoods depended on their fitness, but one or two of the younger ones had over-indulged the day before and rather sheepishly sneaked into her room for black coffee, a couple of aspirins, and to have their legs massaged.

After the practice Davina went home to change and came back at two-thirty to prepare for the match. Almost the first person she saw was Max. He was walking along the corridor with the Chairman, who stopped to ask if she'd had a good Christmas. Davina didn't dare to look at Max but knew that her face had reddened as she answered chokingly, 'Yes, thank you, very good. Did you?'

'Oh, yes, yes. Had all the children and grandchildren round, you know.' He gave her a smiling nod and walked on with Max following. Davina darted a glance at him and saw that Max was trying hard not to laugh. She grinned as she walked past; if only the Chairman had known it, that had been a very leading question!

During the match Davina sat on the trainers' bench in a happy dream, seeing the players running on the field, the advertisements all round the edge and the policemen walking along inside the protective railing, facing the huge and Christmas-noisy crowd, but her thoughts were of Max, high in the Directors' box, or else back at his house and of the hours they had spent in each other's arms.

'You look like a cat who swallowed a whole

bottleful of cream,' Mike Douglas remarked at half-time.

'It's Christmas,' she laughed up at him.

'Don't I know it!' he answered gloomily, looking at his tired players. 'And we've got New Year's Eve to get through next week.'

Davina had left Max's house in such a rush that morning that they had made no plans to meet, so she didn't quite know what to do. She certainly didn't want to hang around the ground after the match and wait for him, because that would let everyone know that the rumours about them were true—even if belatedly. But she wasn't sure whether Max even knew her address or telephone number. She smiled to herself, realising that she was worrying about nothing. If Max wanted her he would find her—and he certainly seemed to want her, more so than ever. So after the match was over and she had dealt with the last cramped muscle, she went back to her flat where she washed her hair and took a long relaxing bath. Afterwards she cooked a special dinner, a dinner for two, sure that he would find her. And he did. The doorbell rang at seven and she ran to answer it. Max stood outside with a big bouquet of red roses in his hand. Red roses in winter! And on Boxing Day too. How on earth had he managed to get them?

He came in and closed the door, then kissed her as if they had been parted for months instead of hours. 'Miss me?' he demanded.

'Certainly not,' she mocked, burying her nose in the flowers. 'Thank you, they're heavenly.'

'Not much of a Christmas present, I'm afraid, but I'll do better when the shops are open.'

Hesitatingly, she said, 'You don't have to buy me presents, Max.'

He kissed her nose. 'I want to. Is that dinner I can smell cooking?' He raised an eyebrow. 'You weren't expecting me, by any chance?'

'I was expecting someone,' Davina admitted teasingly, but saw his eyes start to frown. 'But as Prince Andrew couldn't make it, I suppose I'll just have to make do with you.'

He caught her round the waist. 'Watch it, woman!'

'Why? Don't you like being teased?'

For a moment he looked thoughtful, then gave a slight shrug. 'I suppose I'm just not used to it.'

Davina longed to ask him about his past, about his life with his wife, but she knew it was too soon, much, much too soon.

They had dinner at the table in the sitting room and Max stayed the night, making love to her in her bed, which was only a large single, which made things a whole lot more intimate and meant that they had to sleep closely wrapped in each other's arms all night. For the next three days Davina was on holiday, so they spent it at Max's house, travelling there early the next morning so that Max could feed Buster. They were idyllic days spent roasting chestnuts over the fire, walking and talking, but mostly making love. And with each day, Max's step seemed to become lighter, the lines to ease around his mouth and eyes. Davina teased him and made him laugh, even once made him chase her through the woods until he caught her and kissed her in a sudden fever of aroused passion, the dog barking excitedly around them and then wandering off as they completely ignored

him. Davina was happy in the heady power she
found she had to arouse him, to make him groan
as she gently explored his body, finding out the
things that pleased him most. She was happy, too,
when he talked about himself, although he didn't
do so very often, telling her of his youth or the
places he had been to. But he never mentioned his
wife, and she began to feel that the hurt was still
raw even after three years. How he must have
loved her, then.

For a moment jealousy consumed her, but
Davina fought it back. She mustn't get possessive
about him, she mustn't.

On the Saturday she had to work again, and
while she was at the Club Max went out and
bought her an expensive gold bracelet. He gave it
to her that night, after dinner, fastening it on her
wrist himself.

'It—It's beautiful,' Davina murmured, her voice
rather chokey.

'A belated Christmas present,' he said lightly,
his lips curled into an amused smile as he looked
at her.

'You shouldn't have.'

'Why not?' The amusement was clear in his
voice.

She was silent for a moment looking down at
the bracelet gleaming on her wrist. 'It makes me
feel like a mistress.'

He laughed. 'I thought that was what you were
going to say. Idiot! It's only a Christmas present.'
And he sat on the settee, pulling her down on to
his lap.

'I haven't given you anything,' she objected,
slightly mollified.

'Oh, yes, you have—more than you'll ever know. But of course, if you'd like to add to your present . . .' And he raised his eyebrows suggestively.

She gave him a playful punch on the jaw. 'You're insatiable!'

'And I'm very fortunate in being able to say the same about you.' He kissed her, leaning her back against the arm of the settee, but when he went to unbutton her blouse, she stopped him, knowing she would never be able to think of anything else once he started fondling her. Getting rather agitatedly to her feet, she walked over to the fire and stood looking into the flames, then she said, 'Do you—do you mind if I ask you something?'

Max ran a hand through his hair and looked at her with a slight frown in his eyes. 'I don't mind you asking, but I don't guarantee to answer it,' he said rather brusquely.

Gripping her hands together, Davina said, 'You said you wanted me from the moment you first saw me. Was that true or just—just something you said?'

'No, it was quite true,' he answered, watching her intently.

'Was it because—I reminded you of your wife?' she asked painfully.

She waited tensely for his reply, still gazing into the fire, her nerves on edge, wondering what he would say, whether he would lie or tell the truth, whether she would know. But Max astounded her completely by beginning to laugh. Incredulously she swung to face him and saw that he had thrown his head back and was indulging in rich masculine laughter. 'My dear girl! What on earth put that idea into your head?' he demanded, his shoulders shaking. 'You're not in the least like her.' Getting to his feet, he came over and put his hands on her arms, looking earnestly into her face. 'I wanted you because you're tall and slim and blonde and lovely. Because you curve in all the right places and you have a way of walking that knocks me out. When you strode into the boardroom at the Club with that challenging air about you it was as if someone had punched me in the stomach.'

'But you didn't want me for the job. And you tried to get rid of me,' Davina protested.

His hands tightened on her arms. 'I know. Because I didn't want to get involved. I didn't want to . . .' He paused, searching for words. 'You had such an effect on me that I knew it might lead to—well, this, and at the time I didn't want it. I wasn't ready for it.'

'But you are now?'

He laughed shortly and tweaked a lock of her hair. 'It seems that chemistry is more powerful than common sense.' He felt Davina stiffen under his hands and said quickly, 'Sorry, that wasn't very well put, was it? It wasn't meant to slight you in any way. You've made me very happy—the happiest I've been in years.'

Davina looked at him curiously. 'If you didn't want to get involved with a woman, couldn't you still have found someone, just for a night or two?'

Max's eyebrows rose and he pretended to be shocked so that she would blush. 'Davina! What are you suggesting?' Then he shook his head. 'The idea didn't appeal. I was waiting for a choice bird like you to come along.'

Davina chuckled and put her arms round his

neck, moving against him provocatively. 'But you had opportunities.'

'A few,' he admitted modestly. 'Women seem to think that there's only one way a widower can be comforted.'

Leaning back against his hands, she pushed her hips against his and immediately felt his body harden. 'Would you like some comfort now?' she offered.

His hands tightened, digging into her flesh. 'Now there,' he said unsteadily, 'is an offer no man in his right mind could refuse.' And he laid her down beside him on the rug.

The next morning there was a thick frost on the ground. Davina looked out of the window, shivered, and got back under the duvet, glad it was Sunday.

'I like seeing you walk around the room naked,' Max told her. 'I've a good mind to take your clothes away and make you do it all the time.'

Davina cheekily put out the tip of her tongue at him and he immediately grabbed her and kissed her hard. 'Do you realise it's New Year's Eve?' she said when she was allowed to speak again. 'What shall we do to celebrate?'

'I can think of several very pleasant ways,' Max said with a grin, but then frowned. 'Oh, hell, I forgot—I've been invited to a party by Sir Reginald's sister. How about you? Have you been invited anywhere?'

'There's a big dance at the Town Hall. I was going to that with a party of friends. But I'd much rather spend the evening with you.'

Max groaned. 'So would I. I shall resent every hour I'm away from you.'

'Do you have to go?' Davina asked wistfully.

'Afraid so. There's a dinner first and I've been invited to that too. It would be extremely rude of me not to turn up.'

'Couldn't you say you were ill or something?' she wheedled.

He laughed. 'Jezebel!' But then he shook his head. 'We'll just have to have our own party here beforehand.'

Davina hesitated, but couldn't resist asking, 'Couldn't you—take me with you?'

Max sat up and looked at her contemplatively. 'Just what are you saying, Davina?'

She bit her lip, then sat up beside him, the intimacy of lying together lost. Pulling the duvet up to cover herself, she said uncertainly, 'I want to know what—what our relationship is now.'

'We're lovers,' he said shortly. 'We enjoy going to bed together.'

Davina's fingers tightened on the duvet. 'And is that all?'

'Isn't that enough for now?' he countered.

Picking her words, she said carefully, 'I enjoy being with you, too. It isn't just sex.'

'And I with you. But don't you think that it's rather soon to commit ourselves?'

She shook her head but couldn't look at him. 'Not for me, it isn't.' Adding, 'The people at the Club were talking about us even before—this week. If they know already . . .'

'There's a world of difference between suspecting something or knowing it for a fact. No, I prefer to keep things the way they are at the moment.'

Her face hardened. 'Why?' she demanded bitterly. 'Because you're ashamed of me? Because

I'm not good enough to mix with your friends, is that it?' Pushing the covers aside, she moved to jump out of bed, but Max grabbed her and pulled her back.

'Don't be so damn stupid,' he said angrily. 'Of course I'm not ashamed of you. I'm proud that you came to me, that we're lovers. But I'm not ready to ... Davina, I envy your sureness, but please don't expect me to be the same. Not so soon. Not after only a week. Let's go on keeping it to ourselves for a while yet.'

'You mean meet in secret, not even go out together like ordinary people?'

'Of course we can go out together. But don't push me, Davina. There's plenty of time.'

There was a note in his voice that warned her not to say any more, so she allowed him to pull her down into bed again and kiss and caress her, and soon she forgot everything but the touch of his hands on her skin and the unquenchable fire Max aroused in her as he expertly made love to her.

In the afternoon they drank champagne and wished each other a happy new year. 'And it will be a wonderful year for us, darling,' Max promised as he clinked his glass against hers.

'Of course,' she agreed, but when she left him to drive home she couldn't but wish it were otherwise. She really knew very little more about him than she had at the beginning, only that there was no way he was going to commit himself to her. And if she pushed him she would lose him. Maybe she shouldn't have said anything. Maybe he was right and it was too soon. But her spirit rebelled at a furtive, hole-and-corner affair. Why couldn't they

be like any other couple and start being seen
around together? Or was it that Max had
ambitions beyond her? Sir Reginald's sister, for
example. Davina remembered her from the Club
dance, looking so sophisticated and holding on to
Max's arm with such a possessive air, as if she was
already sure of him. But Max had never been to
bed with her, Davina was at least certain of that.
He had no reason to say that it had been years if it
hadn't been true. But he still hadn't even told her
why it was that he hadn't wanted to get involved
with her or why he didn't want to commit himself
now. As far as Davina was concerned going to bed
with him was a commitment in itself, by giving
herself to him she was forming what was to her a
serious relationship. But it seemed with Max that
it wasn't so; he still wanted to be free to walk away
if he wanted to, even though he needed her so
badly.

She enjoyed the party that evening as much as
anyone could whose thoughts were elsewhere, and
welcomed the new year in with cheers and kisses
all round. Giles Allinson and Elaine were there, and
so was her ex-boy-friend Peter with another girl.
Davina was glad Peter had found someone else,
but she hated being on her own and wished Max
was with her. But being alone meant that she was
also an onlooker for some of the time, and
watching this crowd of contemporaries, people she
had grown up with, made her realise that their
noisy celebration probably wasn't Max's scene.
She could imagine him at the Chairman's sister's,
having a sedate dinner and then just standing
around socialising until champagne was brought
round to see in the new year. She sighed and took

a long swallow of her drink. His world seemed light years away from hers, so maybe he was right. Maybe they weren't compatible. In anything but sex, that was. They were more than compatible there!

'Penny for them,' said Peter, coming up to her. 'What's the matter, Davy? You don't look very happy.'

'Nonsense, I'm fine,' she disagreed with a laugh.

'I tried to phone you two or three times last week, but I couldn't get hold of you. Did you go to your parents after all?'

'No. I—er—went to stay with a friend. What did you want to speak to me about?' she asked quickly before he could pursue it.

'My parents are having everyone round for drinks tomorrow lunchtime and they wanted to know if you'd like to come.'

'Tomorrow?' Davina was about to refuse so that she could be with Max, but then she hesitated; if Max wanted to be a free agent then she had the right to be one too. 'Thanks, I'd love to come. About midday?'

'Yes, any time after twelve.' Peter looked at her speculatively. 'What are these rumours I've been hearing about you from Giles? He said you're supposed to be having an affair with one of the Directors of the Rovers.'

Davina laughed lightly. 'Oh, that's just because I got stuck there in the fog one night. Mr Blair left his wallet behind at the Club and I took it out to him.' She raised her eyebrows at him. 'Really, Peter, can you see me with someone like that?'

He nodded, suddenly serious. 'Yes, I could. I

always thought you had class, that you would get somewhere.'

'Thanks,' Davina said sincerely, and touched his hand. 'But being physio to the Rovers is the height of my ambition.'

'Come on, you two!' someone called out, and they were pulled into a long conga line that snaked out into the street and all round the hall.

Deliberately Davina left the phone off the hook and slept late the next morning, not getting up until it was time to get ready and go over to Peter's parents' house. She put the receiver back on just before she left and it almost immediately began to ring. Davina hesitated, then left it ringing.

It was a jolly crowd, full of laughter about last night's celebrations, the room packed tight with people, the drink plentiful. Most of the people drifted away by about four, but there were still twenty or so left who stayed to play silly games and then have supper, so it was nearly midnight before Davina got back home. She parked in the car park at the front of the block and got rather tiredly out of the car; two nights of celebrations on top of a week of hectic lovemaking was beginning to take its toll. She turned to lock the car, but then her arm was caught in a tight grip and Max swung her round to face him. 'Where the hell have you been?' he demanded curtly. 'I've been trying to get hold of you all day.'

'Well, now you have got hold of me, haven't you?' Davina answered rather breathlessly. 'Literally.'

His grip tightened for a moment. 'Let's go up to your flat,' he said grimly.

Silently they walked together into the main entrance and rode up in the lift, his hand still on her arm as if he was afraid she would try to run away. Davina took out her key and unlocked the door and as soon as they were inside Max slammed it shut. His eyes angry, he repeated, 'Where have you been all day?'

Trying to keep her voice calm, she said, 'To a party.'

'All day? You couldn't have been. Where was it?'

'At a friend's house. It started as lunchtime drinks and just kept going.'

'And I don't suppose it occurred to you to pick up a phone and let me know where you were, did it?' he said, his voice full of biting sarcasm.

She raised her head angrily. 'Just what is this, Max, some sort of inquisition? You can't have it both ways. Either we—we mean something to each other or we don't.'

'So that's it; you're trying to blackmail me.'

'*No!* No, I'm not. I just want to know where I stand. What I am. Am I your girl-friend or—or just someone you keep shut away in a cupboard and only take out whenever you want sexual satisfaction?' she asked baldly. 'Because if so I want to be free to live my own life.'

Max glared at her, his hands clenched. 'And I suppose being free means that you can go out with other men?'

Davina's eyes closed for a second and she took a deep breath, her nails digging into her palms. 'I don't want other men. I only want you. Surely you know that? It's the other way round. You don't want to be—tied down, I suppose you'd call it.'

'Do you want me to marry you, is that it?'

Her voice shook. 'Not—not unless you love me.'

'I want you. I—can't feel anything beyond that,' he admitted gruffly, turning away.

Silly tears pricked her eyes, but Davina blinked them back. 'Can't? That's a strange word to use.'

Swinging round, Max came over and caught her wrists. 'Oh, God, Davina, what the hell are we rowing for? I'm crazy about you, isn't that enough?' Suddenly his hands were at her clothes, pulling them off. 'Today's been one of the longest in my life. I've been sitting outside, waiting for you to come home for hours.' His mouth was on her neck, kissing her avidly as he undid her bra and took it off, then his fingers were on the zipper of her trousers, pulling it down.

'Max, no.' But her half-hearted protest was too late anyway as he picked her up and carried her into the bedroom, barely giving himself time to take off his own clothes before he made love to her with a fierce passion fuelled by anger, taking her with a forceful strength he had never used with her before. He made Davina gasp and cry out, her hands gripping the rails of the bedhead as her body arched in deep and prolonged ecstasy.

Afterwards they lay in mutual exhaustion. Max still on top of her. 'Promise me,' he said urgently. 'Promise me you'll never do that to me again.'

Turning her head so that she could kiss him, Davina put her hands in his thick dark hair. 'I promise,' she whispered, her breathing still uneven. 'I'm sorry.' Then she opened her mouth under his.

That night was almost like the first they had spent together; neither of them tired of making love, each fired by the knowledge that they had come close to a fight. But in some ways tonight was better because they had learned how to please each other, or rather Davina had learnt how to please Max, because he had always known where to touch and kiss her to lift her into giddy excitement.

When morning came, Max went back to his own house while Davina drove to work, and this set the pattern of the next few weeks. They spent almost every night together, at Davina's flat during the week and at Max's house at the weekends. They never arrived at the Club or left together, and didn't see more of one another there than they had previously. Max kept his promise and often took her out, but always to a restaurant in the country somewhere or to a concert or the theatre in the next big town, almost twenty-five miles away, where he wasn't known. Once the team played an away match where they all again stayed overnight in a hotel. Davina lay in bed, hoping Max would come to her, but felt no surprise, only bitter disappointment, when he didn't.

After that her lovemaking assumed a fevered kind of urgency, because she knew it wasn't going to last, that this wonderful thing they shared between them was going to be lost through Max's refusal to commit himself to the relationship. In some ways it heightened the exquisite pleasure of being held in his arms and of willingly, almost greedily, offering her body to his dominant masculinity, because she never knew how long it would go on, whether this night might be the last they would spend together.

January and then February passed, without any lessening of their physical need for each other, but to Davina the strain of living such an existence was beginning to become unbearable. In early March she asked for a couple of days' holiday so that she could travel down to Kent after the Saturday match and spend a long weekend with her parents.

'Must you go?' Max asked when she told him, then answered his own question. 'Yes, I suppose you must. I'm afraid I've monopolised you too much.'

'You can come with me, if you like,' Davina said with studied casualness. 'My parents' house is big enough. And you could even bring Buster with you.'

'Thanks, but I think I'll take the opportunity to go to Geneva on business. I've been intending to go for some time.'

She turned away to hide the hurt in her eyes. 'I'll be back on the Wednesday morning.'

Coming up behind her, Max slid his arms round her waist and buried his face in her hair, then began to kiss her neck. 'What would you like me to bring you back from Geneva?'

Davina bit her lip hard and closed her eyes, leaning her head back against his shoulder. 'Perfume would be nice,' she answered after a moment, hoping he would mistake the unsteadiness in her voice for desire.

'Perfume it shall be. I shall miss you.' His fingers went to the buttons on her blouse, undid them and slipped inside. 'God, Davina, you're beautiful,' he groaned. 'I only have to look at you and I want you.'

She took a deep breath and turned to him. 'Why don't you take me, then?'

Max's eyes lit. He smiled, and did as she'd invited.

It was a long drive from Redford to Kent and Davina was tired by the time she got there. She had supper with her parents and chatted to them afterwards for an hour, but then went up to bed. Her mother followed her to her room a few minutes later with a hot milk drink which she put down on the bedside cabinet, then she turned to look at her daughter. 'You're thinner,' she observed.

'I do some exercising with the team sometimes; it keeps me fit.'

'And you're not happy, I can see that. What is it, your job?' And when Davina shook her head, 'A man, then?'

'Yes, a man. But I don't want to talk about it. I just want to think things out. That's why I came down here, to give myself some breathing space.'

Her mother nodded understandingly. 'All right, but if you feel you need to talk to someone, your father and I are always willing to listen.' She turned to go, then paused at the door. 'I suppose he's already married.'

Davina shook her head. 'No.'

'Then why is there a problem?'

'Oh, Mum, *I just wish I knew!*'

The weather was warm and almost springlike during the next three days and Davina was able to go and work in the garden or drive the two miles to the coast and walk along the empty beaches, her hair blowing in the sea breeze. She knew that the time had come when she had to make a decision; whether she was willing to go on indefinitely with Max the way things were and live more or less as his clandestine mistress, to put it at its crudest, always hoping he would change, or whether to end it now, make a clean break and have nothing more to do with him; never again have him touch her or have his hard body lift her to the heights of ecstasy. Common sense told her she must finish it *now*, but her body rejected that decision utterly.

Sitting down in the shelter of a sand dune, Davina tried desperately to force herself to make the right decision, but she knew that either way led to unhappiness. So would it be better to be unhappy with him or without him? There was only one answer to that, but she knew it wouldn't be the right one in the long run. She squared her shoulders and made herself face reality. So if she left him, what then? She would also have to leave Redford and go away somewhere where he couldn't find her; for she was quite sure he would come after her and use her physical need for him to make her come back, because he knew that he only had to kiss and touch her and she wouldn't be able to resist him. So she would have to go a long way away, emigrate to Australia or something. Or perhaps she could go and visit her brother, who was working in Saudi Arabia, for a few months.

Another thought occurred to her. Maybe she might not have to go away. If she just told Max that she was leaving it might make him realise just what he was losing and force him into making a decision. But that was moral blackmail and she shrank away from it. But at the end of the three days she had decided that that was what she would try. She felt she owed herself the chance that it might work.

She travelled back to Redford early on Wednesday morning and went straight to the Club, where Max phoned her later in the day to say he would pick her up at seven to take her out to dinner.

She dressed very carefully that evening, washing her hair so that it shone in soft curls around her head and shoulders and putting on a blue dress that clung down to her knees and then flared out into a deep frill round the bottom. It was a very sexy dress, a new one, the kind that she would normally only have worn to a party, but tonight she wanted to look sexy. After putting on her make-up Davina went over to the bedside cabinet and took out her jewellery box. Max had been more than generous to her and there were now several pieces of jewellery there. Now she put all the pieces on; the necklace with matching earrings, the gold bracelet and a pretty butterfly clip for her hair. The only thing missing was a ring. He had never bought her one of those, although he had bought her lots of other things too: flowers, chocolates, accessories; he seldom came empty-handed, making Davina feel more like a mistress with every gift.

He arrived promptly at seven and raised his eyebrows when he saw her, his gaze running appreciatively over her tall slim figure, smiling because he knew exactly what was underneath. 'You look stunning!' he exclaimed in admiration. 'Is this some special celebration?'

'Well, it is the longest we've been parted.'

'Mm, and I missed you.' He took her in his arms

and kissed her. 'I could almost wish we were staying in tonight.'

'But I'm hungry,' Davina protested. 'And we can always come back early.'

'Is that a promise? Oh, I have a present for you.' He took a box of expensive French perfume from his pocket. 'And I thought you might like this.'

'This' proved to be a thin gold chain with a tiny heart dangling from it. Davina took it slowly. 'It's lovely. Thank you.'

'Do you know what it is?'

She looked at it more closely and realised that it was too small to be a necklace but too large to be a bracelet.

'It's an ankle chain,' he told her with a grin. 'All the girls in Geneva are wearing them. Here, let me put it on for you.'

Davina looked at him for a moment, then lifted her foot up on to a chair. Max fastened the chain in place but kept hold of her ankle. 'You have beautiful legs,' he told her. 'All your body is beautiful. I can't wait to make love to you again.'

Her nails digging into her palm, Davina managed to lean forward and playfully smack his hands. 'Unhand me, mister! I want my dinner.'

He laughed and helped her into her thick white wool coat. 'Why don't you let me buy you a fur coat? I'm sure you can't be warm enough in this.'

'Of course I am. Don't be silly. How would I explain a fur coat?'

They drove out to a country club which they'd been to a couple of times before, the kind of place that had dim lighting and a tiny dance floor where you could smooch around between courses. The kind of out-of-town place where executives could take their secretaries without their wives finding out about it. Davina ate very little, full of mingled anticipation, dread, and rising anger. They danced only a couple of times and left almost immediately after the meal, Max often putting his hand on her thigh in nerve-tingling anticipation as they drove back to her flat.

Once there, Davina took off her coat, putting on only a couple of lamps to light the room. Then she turned to Max. 'Don't you want to undress me?' she asked huskily.

Max's breath caught in his throat and he strode quickly towards her. 'Darling!'

His hand went to the back of her dress, but she said, 'I think you'd better take all this jewellery off first.'

He did so, finishing with the ankle chain.

'There, now I don't feel so much like a Christmas tree,' Davina said lightly. 'No, put the jewellery in your pocket,' she added as he went to put the things on a nearby table.

Max raised his eyebrows. 'Why in my pocket?'

'Because you'll be taking it with you when you go,' she answered, keeping her voice as level as she could.

'Take it . . .!' He became very still. 'What are you saying?'

'That after tonight I don't want to see you again. In the morning you can take all the things you've given me and leave.'

His jaw hardened. 'You know you don't mean that!'

'Yes, I do, Max. I thought it over very carefully during the weekend and I've made up my mind.'

Max dropped the jewellery on the table and

thrust his hands into his pockets as if he didn't trust himself not to get hold of her. 'And just what made you reach this momentous decision?' he asked sardonically.

Davina gulped, but her chin came up. 'Because I'm tired of being treated like some kind of plaything, like a doll that's shut away in a cupboard all day and only taken out at night when you take me to bed with you.'

He laughed. 'That's ridiculous! I . . .'

But she went on, her voice rising, 'I don't want to be just a mistress, to be given presents instead of love. To be taken to places where you're not known in case we're seen together. Tell me, Max, just what do you think would happen if someone *did* see us? It wouldn't be the end of the world, would it? Or would it be the end for us? Would you drop me rather than face up to having to commit yourself to me?'

'Davina, this is silly. We're happy as we are.'

'No. No, I'm not happy, Max. Can't you even see that? This situation isn't right for me. I'm not—I'm not a tramp.'

He stepped quickly across and put his hands on her arms. 'Of course you're not,' he said roughly. 'Don't ever think that.'

'But I do, because that's the way you make me feel. Oh, a high class one, if you like, but by giving me these presents you make me feel as if I'm selling myself to you. Or that you're paying for something which I offered to you freely, first out of desire and need, and then out of love.'

His hands tightened and then he let her go. 'Are you saying that you're in love with me?' he demanded harshly.

'I would hardly have gone on with this for so long if I wasn't! Is loving you such a terrible thing?' she asked desperately.

He turned away so that she couldn't see his face. 'If all you want me to do is stop giving you presents . . .'

'Oh, Max! Why won't you understand? Won't you even tell me what it is that's made you so afraid to let yourself love me? Was it your wife who made you like this?'

He turned to her, his face a tight mask. 'That's none of your damn business.'

Davina flinched as if he'd struck her hard across the face. Her hands went up to the zip of her dress and she began to tug it down.

'What are you doing?' he demanded.

'I'm taking my clothes off so that I can pay for my dinner,' she said bitterly. 'How would you like me? You're paying.'

'For God's sake!' Max caught her wrists and pulled them down. 'What do you want from me?'

'I want you to acknowledge the fact that we have a relationship.'

'By marrying you, is that it?' he demanded harshly.

Her voice breaking, Davina said, 'I want to marry you, Max. I want it more than anything else in the world. But if you don't want to, then I'm willing to settle for less. For just living together. As long as we do it openly—not keep it like some furtive affair.'

His hand went to her neck and he began to stroke it with his thumb, his touch sending sensuous shivers down her spine. 'I could make you take all that back. I could make you agree to keep things as they are. I could make you beg me to. I need only start to make love to you.'

'I know,' she admitted on a sob. 'But you wouldn't make me *feel* differently.'

For a moment his hand tightened on her throat. 'So if I don't agree to what you want, it's goodbye, is that it?'

'Yes.' It was the hardest word she'd ever had to say.

'Do you realise that's moral blackmail?' He looked into her eyes. 'Yes, I see you do.' He let her go and stepped away. 'You should know me better than to think I'd succumb to blackmail, Davina. When you change your mind you'll know where to find me.'

That 'when' angered her. 'Don't forget to take back your presents,' she reminded him stiffly.

He looked down at the small heap of jewellery on the table. 'Keep it. And wear it when you come to tell me you've changed your mind. All of it!' And he strode out of the flat, slamming the door behind him.

CHAPTER EIGHT

THE next morning Davina carefully packed the
jewellery and other things Max had given her into
a parcel and sent it to his house by registered post.
She went on with her life as best she could,
working, eating and sleeping, but it was largely
automatic. She didn't go out and couldn't even
concentrate on reading or watching the TV. Her
life felt completely empty, especially at night when
her body craved for his and she lay awake and
miserable in her lonely bed.

Max didn't seem to come to the Club at all, or if
he did she didn't see him. She waited for him to
call, to realise that he really needed her. But
although she was at home every evening and
looked eagerly on her desk for a letter from him at
the Club, the days passed without any word. It
made her wretched but angry, too. Did he really
expect her to eat dirt and beg him to take her
back? It seemed that he did, as the days stretched
into weeks and the only time she saw him was at
the match on the second Saturday afternoon when
she looked up from the field into the Directors'
box way above her.

After waiting three weeks, Davina wrote off for
a job she saw advertised in the *Physio* magazine. It
was as an assistant physio at a big sports complex
in Sydney, Australia. Which was just about as far
away as she could possibly get from Max.

The weather, which had been quite mild,

changed with a vengeance and there was frost and snow, followed by heavy continuous rain for several days. The Rovers' pitch was well drained and didn't get waterlogged, but they had to play two matches on it in a week and it got extremely muddy. It was getting towards the end of the season now and the team were doing well, but they had only managed to draw in the current round of the F.A. Cup and had to have a replay on the Wednesday evening. The fans weren't so happy about this because it meant they had to queue up and pay for extra tickets, and the team could well have done without it; they had worked hard and needed a longer break between matches to recover.

On the Wednesday afternoon, Davina ran from her car through the rain, and into the stadium. The weather, she thought, as she walked to her therapy room, was about as miserable as she was. After hanging up her coat, she got the couch ready for her first patient. She had three players to see this afternoon, all of whom were reporting for fitness tests to see if they could play in tonight's game. It was a part of her job she didn't like very much because the players' careers depended so much on their being able to play as often as possible, especially in a game like tonight's which was so important for the Club and which was also being televised and would be seen by millions of people. Sometimes, she knew, they deliberately made light of their injuries or pretended they were completely better when they weren't, just because they were so anxious to play. But Davina was experienced enough to know when someone was lying to her and she hadn't let any of them get away with it.

Someone knocked on the door and she looked up, expecting her first patient, but Giles Allinson came in.

'Hallo. You're not on my list. Or have you done something I don't know about?'

He grinned widely. 'I have, but not what you mean. I've asked Elaine to marry me.'

'Wow! That was fast work. I expect she turned you down,' she added mischievously.

'Certainly not. She knows a good thing when she sees it.'

'Chauvinist!' Davina laughed. 'But seriously, many congratulations. I hope you'll both be very happy.'

'Of course we will,' he boasted, his confidence way up. 'And we're having a party at Elaine's place on Saturday night to celebrate. You're invited, of course, and bring a boy-friend if you want to. And I think Elaine has something to ask you—something about being a bridesmaid.'

'A bridesmaid?' Davina blinked and tried hard to keep smiling. 'Oh, I don't know . . .'

'But of course you must. Elaine and I owe you a lot. If it hadn't been for you we would never have met.'

She didn't want to be a bridesmaid, she wanted to be a bride. Max's bride. But somehow Davina swallowed the bitterness in her throat and smiled. 'Thanks. Of course I'll be your bridesmaid.'

'Great! We're having the wedding at the beginning of June, as soon as the season's finished.'

There was another knock on the door and her first patient came in, so Giles went away. After giving him some tests she passed the player as fit to play, but was a bit dubious about the second. 'The leg is nearly as good as new, but the conditions are so bad out on the pitch that I'm going to recommend you as a reserve—fit to play but only if needed. Okay?'

'Fair enough,' the man agreed. 'At least I'll be part of the match.'

Her third patient was the problem, as Davina had known he would be. A young player who had only signed with the Rovers at the beginning of the season for one year, Gary Redmond had hurt his knee a few weeks ago and was desperate to get back into the game, always afraid he might lose his one golden opportunity to make good. He tried to make light of his injury when he came in, vaulting easily up on to the couch.

'How is it today?' Davina asked him.

'Fine. Can't feel a thing.'

Davina had been giving him therapy every day and the knee was much better, but she knew he was lying. She pressed his knee experimentally and felt him stiffen so that he wouldn't show any pain. She already knew the result, but put him through all the tests anyway, then she said, 'I'm sorry, Gary, but it isn't healed enough. Give it another week of treatment and maybe you'll be fit enough for next Saturday.'

'What d'you mean, not fit enough? Of course I'm fit. Look!' And he jumped up and down.

'That isn't doing you any good. And I did warn you . . .'

'I'm all right, I tell you,' he shouted, losing his temper. 'You stupid bitch! You're no bloody good. Why don't they get someone who knows

what they're doing? You damn well tell them I'm
fit to play!'

Davina walked to the door and opened it.
'You're not fit, Gary. I'm sorry.'

He started to yell and scream abuse at her,
calling her names that made her cheeks burn with
anger and embarrassment. Davina went out into
the corridor and began to walk towards Mike
Douglas's office, but Gary still came after her,
swearing at her, using words she'd never even
heard before. Some players came from the
gymnasium and then Mike Douglas came out of
his office—followed by Max. 'What the hell's all
the shouting about?' Mike demanded.

'It's that stinking slut that calls herself a physio!'
Gary yelled, completely out of control. 'The stupid
tart doesn't know what she's talking about. All
she's good for is . . .'

'That's enough!' Max's voice broke through
Gary's just as Mike Douglas stepped angrily
forward and got hold of him.

'If Davina says you're not fit then you're not,'
Mike told him roundly, propelling him back into
the therapy room. Davina followed and Max came
in behind her and shut the door.

Her cheeks were still burning and she was
trembling, but she wasn't concerned with Gary
any more, she was only aware of Max. She turned
to look at him, her eyes wide and intense.

'Did he touch you?' he asked brusquely.

'No.' She shook her head.

Max's face looked drawn and the lines she had
kissed away from around his mouth had started to
come back. Oh Max, her heart cried out. You fool!
Don't do this to us. But he turned away and spoke

to Gary Redmond, his voice scathing. 'If you can't control your temper we don't want you in this Club. If you can lose it with someone like Davina who has been doing her best to help you, then you can lose it on the field. There are enough good players, we don't need a spoiled brat who can't accept the decision of an expert. This incident will go before the Board on Monday morning for them to decide what disciplinary measures they want to take. In the meantime you will leave the Club grounds at once and not return until you're sent for. Is that understood?'

Gary glared at him in surly defiance. 'I knew *you'd* take her side. Everyone knows she's your dolly bird—your bit on the side,' he said insultingly.

Max's face went white and he took a hasty step towards him, but Mike Douglas quickly stepped between them and muttered to Gary, 'You stupid young fool! Get out. Fast.' And taking him by the arm, he marched the player out of the room.

Davina stood very still, her hands clenched, not looking at Max. 'How the hell did he find out?' he demanded angrily.

'I don't know.' She shook her head hopelessly, knowing that now people knew about them it was indeed over. Max would never come back to her now; he would probably accuse her of telling everyone herself to try and force him into it. So to forestall him, she said sharply, 'You don't have to worry, I won't be an embarrassment to you for much longer. I shall be leaving the Rovers at the end of the season. I've applied for another job.'

For a moment he was silent, only the tightness

of his jaw betraying any emotion. 'Where?' he asked at length.

Davina laughed, a harsh, mirthless sound. 'Oh, far enough away for no one in Redford to ever hear of me again. You'll soon be able to live down our sordid little affair.'

'It wasn't like that,' Max said tightly.

'No, but that's what you've turned it into.' She strode to the door. 'Goodbye, Max.' And she walked out of the room, out of his life, out into the pain of a broken heart.

There was something different about the atmosphere at the Rovers' ground that evening. Perhaps it was because it was dark, the pitch lit by huge floodlights high on their metal pylons. It was a replay of the Cup Final match that the Rovers had drawn against Grantchester United last Saturday with a score of two all, neither side being able to get the better of the other even after extra time. The fans had come in their thousands, both from Redford and by the train and coachload from Grantchester. They sang as usual, waving their scarves and rattles, the red and white of Redford the predominant colours. It was still raining and it was cold, the wind driving the rain so that it stung icily when it hit you. Davina sat on her bench, huddled in sweaters and anorak, looking out at the swaying crowd. There seemed to be a restlessness about them tonight, a sort of pack instinct, probably because this was such an important match. If the Rovers won they would be into the final of the F.A. Cup tournament, and the fans would have all the excitement of the big final at Wembley Stadium in London to anticipate.

But the Grantchester team were good; the crowd were on edge, fanatically willing their team to victory.

The Rovers' management had laid on a brass band for the occasion, but it was so windy that the sound was carried away, the band doing their best but getting so wet that they couldn't read their music, and they marched off to jeers and catcalls from the fans. The teams, however, received huge cheers when they came on and began to warm up, practising goal kicks and passes. The referee called them together and the captains tossed up, Grantchester winning the toss and choosing to play with the wind behind them, although the huge stadium acted almost as a funnel, drawing the wind down and intensifying it, so that it swirled and gave neither side any great advantage. The referee blew his whistle to begin and the crowd roared their encouragement in excited anticipation, the noise deafening. The men began to chase after the ball, the red and white of Redford against the yellow and black of Grantchester, and soon the pitch became a mud-bath, the players sliding all over the place as they strove to control the ball, to score, to please the screaming hordes of spectators.

Davina watched grimly, knowing that in these conditions there were bound to be several injuries on both sides. Why did they do it, she wondered, these young men? For money? For fame? Both, she supposed, but it was far from the glamorous life that most people believed; it was work and guts and strain, an endless endeavour to be fit and on top for as long as possible, before they became too old, sometimes at thirty, to go on. Her first injury came after only fifteen minutes, but she managed to get the man back on his feet and play on, the crowd chanting their impatience while she worked on him. The second injury was to a Grantchester player and she assisted his trainer to take him back to the visitors' changing room, then went back to watch over her own team.

By half-time there had been half a dozen injuries, and Davina spent the time grimly working on twisted ankles, pulled muscles and a cut head where two men had collided. 'This is ridiculous!' she said angrily to Mike Douglas. 'Can't you stop the game? It isn't fair to ask them to play in these conditions.'

'I'd get torn to pieces if I even suggested it,' Mike answered, but his face, too, was bleak. 'They're not weaklings, Davina; they can take it.'

So the men went back to the sea of mud they laughingly called a pitch, all of them grimly intent on winning, the next forty-five minutes stretching before them like a war, the score still nil–nil and the fans roaring their greed for a goal.

Davina had taken one man off completely and now another went down, so Mike had to send on the man she had passed as fit to be a reserve. She was worried about him, he was one of the older players, all of twenty-eight, and she knew he took more risks than he should to try to keep in the team.

Play went on, if play you could call it, with each side desperately trying to score. There were some near misses but still no goals, and it looked as if the teams would have to play extra time again, another thirty minutes of these terrible conditions. Davina's heart went out to them, but then the

Rovers managed to get hold of the ball, only to have it snatched away just before the goal mouth and sent flying back down the field. It looked as if Grantchester might score, but the injured reserve went charging in, desperately trying to kick it clear. He cannoned into the Grantchester player, the ball for a moment was clear, but then the Rovers' man skidded, unable to stop his wild charge—and accidentally kicked the ball into his own goal! He fell heavily on to his injured leg just as the final whistle blew.

The Rovers' fans went mad. A kind of collective hatred filled them and they came charging on to the pitch like a pack of hungry wolves, roaring insanely. And then Davina was on the pitch and running too, her hat flying off and her hair streaming out behind her as she desperately tried to reach her injured player, who was still lying on the ground, unmoving.

A couple of Rovers' fans in red and white scarves, their hair the bright orange of punks, reached him and began to kick him where he lay. Davina threw herself at them and knocked them out of the way. 'Get away from him! Leave him alone!' But they knocked her aside and began to kick the player again. Her head swimming from the blow, Davina lunged forward and threw herself on top of the player, shielding his body with hers, his head with her arms. More so-called fans had come to surround them and they tried to pull her off, but she held grimly on. So they began to try and kick her out of the way. She felt a boot go into her ribs and cried out, but then the crowd around them began to thin, the hooligans being dragged bodily out of the way, and then Max was there, bending over her, his face a taut mask of fear.

'Davina! Are you hurt? Dear God, what have they done to you?' He dropped to his knees in the mud, and gently pulled her off the injured player, who was still lying unconscious. Mike and some St John Ambulance men came running up with a stretcher, the crowd held back by the police.

Davina saw them through a hazy kind of mist. She heard Max demanding to know who had hit her, his voice raw with fury, and she clung to him as he helped her to her feet. Her legs felt strangely wobbly and she could taste blood in her mouth. 'I'm—I'm all right,' she managed, but Max had to hold her up while they lifted the injured man on to a stretcher and carried him away.

'Can you walk? You're sure you're not hurt?' Max said anxiously, his voice still sharp with fear.

'Oh, I'm fine,' Davina answered him, and promptly passed out into his arms.

She came round in an ambulance and felt a complete fool. Sitting up, she looked at the attendant, who was seeing to the man on the other stretcher. 'How is he?' she asked anxiously.

'He's conscious, but he's obviously done some damage to his leg, so he'll be out of the game for a while. How are you feeling?'

'All right. I shouldn't be here—I only fainted.'

'Best to let the doctors have a look at you, though. I hear you saved this chap from being kicked to pieces,' he added, admiration in his voice.

At the hospital they were taken into the outpatients' department, where the doctor said her ribs had been bruised but not broken. 'You're a lucky girl,' he told her. 'It could have been a lot worse.' Davina agreed with him, until she saw herself in the mirror and realised that she was going to have a beautiful black eye. She put her mud-soaked clothes back on and went out to Reception, wondering how she was supposed to get home. But Max was there. He got up from his seat beside Mike and strode quickly towards her, taking her hands.

'Are you all right?' he asked urgently.

She smiled. 'Yes, I really am fine this time.' She looked down at their joined hands. 'Do you think you ought to do that? Someone might see.'

'Then they can see this as well.' And Max took her in his arms to kiss her, deeply and lingeringly.

'Oh, Max,' Davina breathed when he at last let her go. 'Oh, Max!' And she burst into tears.

He laughed. 'That wasn't quite the reaction I expected! Here, take my handkerchief.' He led her over to Mike and she sat down, but kept a tight hold of his hand.

Mike grinned at them. 'I wondered how long it would be before you two realised you had something going for you. You argued so much you had to be in love!

Max gave him a rueful grin. 'So it seems. Look, Mike, I'm going to take Davina home. Will you stay on here until the player comes out of X-Ray?'

'Yes, of course.'

'I ought to stay too,' Davina demurred. 'He might need me to . . .'

'No, he won't,' Max told her firmly, and he put his arm round her waist and led her out of the hospital.

'I can walk, you know,' she told him, but made

no attempt to draw away. He merely looked at her and she smiled happily, leaning against him. He put her into his Rolls and drove to her flat.

'I collected your bag from the Club. If you'll give me your key I'll go up and pack some things for you.'

'Where are we going?'

'My place.' But then he collected himself. 'Our place.'

Quickly she looked at him and saw the love and tenderness in his eyes. It was all right, everything was going to be all right. 'Oh, Max!' And she began to cry again.

He leant forward and kissed her. 'Stop crying, woman. I'm running out of handkerchiefs!'

That made her laugh and she gave him her key, waiting until he quickly returned with a small suitcase. 'We can collect the rest of your things later. Now I want to get you home.'

When they got to the house he took her upstairs to the bathroom, where he took off her filthy clothes, exclaiming with furious anger when he saw the red bruises on her legs and ribs. 'Those louts! If I get my hands on them . . .'

'It's nothing,' Davina soothed. 'Nothing now.'

He bathed her with his own hands, and afterwards gently dried her, then kissed each bruise as she stood there, her body trembling, her eyes darkly sensuous. He found a long white nightdress and put it on her, then carried her into his bedroom and laid her in the bed. 'Are you hungry?' he asked.

Davina shook her head. 'No.' She smiled. 'You got pretty muddy too.'

He looked ruefully down at his trousers. 'I did,

didn't I? My turn to shower and change. I won't be long.'

But she caught his hand. 'Max, I want to thank you for coming when you did at the match. For knocking those hooligans away.'

His hand tightened on hers until his grip hurt. 'My darling girl! When I saw you go down under that mob . . .' His voice broke, too full of emotion to go on. He let her go and walked abruptly from the room.

When he came back twenty minutes or so later he was carrying a bottle of champagne and a couple of glasses and he was wearing pyjamas, which made Davina laugh, because they'd never bothered with them before. 'Champagne and demure night clothes,' she mocked. 'I feel as if it ought to be my wedding night!'

Max got into bed beside her, opened the champagne and poured it. 'Not quite yet.' He kissed her on the nose. 'We'll wait till your black eye recovers first.'

She looked at him, her eyes wide, and said faintly, 'I think you just proposed to me.'

He grinned. 'Yes, I think I did. Don't you dare start crying again,' he added quickly.

Davina laughed shakily. 'Definitely not!'

'Good.' He raised his glass. 'To us.' And after he'd drunk the toast he leaned over to kiss her. 'I've missed you,' he said huskily. 'More than I could ever have thought possible.' He kissed her again, then turned away. 'Let's put the TV on.' And he operated the remote control.

'Television?' Davina exclaimed indignantly. 'At a time like this?'

'I want to see if we made the late night news.'

And they had. The all-seeing cameras had captured everything. First there was the commentator describing the Redford player's desperate attempt to save a goal and then the howl of pure rage that went up when the ball went into his own net. Davina watched, tightly holding on to Max's hand, as the fans surged over the barricades and on to the pitch. She saw herself running faster than she'd known she could run and gulped when she saw herself hurl herself at the first two hooligans, then being hit and kicked when she lay on top of the injured man.

'I'll recognise that SOB who hit you,' Max gritted through his teeth. 'And I'll make sure the police find him and throw the book at him!'

But the newsreel had run on and showed Max fighting his way through the crowd to her, literally throwing people out of his way until he reached her, well before anyone else.

Max turned off the set and Davina's hand tightened on his. They were silent for a long moment until Max said, 'I think I just committed myself to you in front of the whole of England.'

Davina leant back against the headboard and brought up her knees to rest her glass on them. 'Would you have otherwise?' she asked, looking down at her glass.

'Oh, yes. I was more than beginning to realise that I was being an utter fool. But you see, the circumstances were—difficult.'

She let out a long breath of heartfelt relief. 'You don't have to tell me—not now.'

'But I think it would be best.' He paused, then said heavily, 'You know my wife was killed in a car smash about three years ago? Well, we hadn't been very happy for some time before that. We married rather young because she had left home and had nowhere to go, but it would have been better if we'd waited. It was all right at first, but as I began to be more successful she became restless, almost jealous. She wanted to start up her own business and to be a career-woman in her own right, and she refused to even consider having children until it got established. It was quite a good idea; she acted as buyer for a lot of small dress shops, going over to France and Italy a lot for them, but it meant that we didn't see much of each other. Her biggest mistake was that she wouldn't delegate, and she wouldn't listen to me when I tried to advise her. She was doing all right and she didn't want to know.

'Then the slump came along and several of the shops went into liquidation owing her a great deal of money. She came to me then to bail her out and I made her promise not to start another business. But then, nearly four years ago, she went into partnership with another woman behind my back and they started a fitness and exercise studio. But she conveniently forgot to tell me about it,' he added bitterly. 'It began to lose money and her partner kept telling her they must invest more, improve the place so that it would pick up, and my wife was fool enough to listen to her; to throw good money after bad. Then her partner sold everything up while she was out of the way and departed with the money. I only found out when I got a polite letter from the bank telling me her account was overdrawn by several thousands.' Max paused, leaning back against the headboard, gazing up at the ceiling. 'That night we had a blazing row—the last in quite a long series. I told her I'd had enough, that I was going to make her an allowance that she could live on quite comfortably, but there wouldn't be any more large sums available because I was going to divorce her. She in return told me what she thought of me and slammed out of the house, driving off in a filthy temper. And drove so badly that she killed herself and came close to killing an innocent lorry-driver.'

'It was definitely an accident?' Davina asked slowly.

Max looked at her. 'Oh, yes. There were witnesses who saw her take a corner too fast and career across the road. The lorry-driver did everything he could to avoid her, but he didn't stand a chance. The police said she'd been drinking, but she kept that hidden from me too.' His voice again grew bitter. 'I vowed then that I'd never marry again. Never commit myself to a woman, especially a business woman, a woman more interested in her career than anything else. I'd learnt a very hard lesson, you see. If you can't trust your wife who can you trust?' He was silent for a couple of minutes and his voice had changed, become lighter, when he said, 'So I kept well clear of women and took up football instead.'

'And that's where I came in.'

'You did indeed. Smashing your way through all my monastic intentions from the moment I saw you walk through the door.'

'I got you below the belt, huh?' Davina said wickedly.

He grinned. 'And some!'

'But you put up quite a fight.'

'Idiot that I was. I've never wanted anyone as badly as I wanted you. As I still want you.'

'So you tried to get me kicked out of the Rovers. I just might not forgive you for that, you know.' Max laughed, sure he was already forgiven. 'I thought you really would have got me the sack after you found out about that letter I wrote to Roger Maynard's wife. But you didn't even tell the Board about it.'

'Yes, I did,' he admitted with a grin. 'It was the best laugh we've had at a Board meeting for years! From that moment you were definitely. in. Sir Reginald even suggested we give you a rise and employ you as a social worker too.'

Davina laughed, then put her glass down and turned towards him. 'And now?' she asked huskily. 'Do I go on working for the Rovers?'

He paused and she could only guess at the effort it cost him to say, 'That must be your decision. You must do what will make you happy.'

'In that case,' she said firmly, 'I'll go on working.' Max's face tightened as he strove to hide his disappointment. But then Davina added teasingly, 'Until the end of the season. And after we're married I think I'll just devote myself to you—and to whatever comes along.'

He sat up straight and stared at her. 'Do you mean that? Yes,' he said, looking into her eyes, 'I really believe you do. Oh, my love. My darling!' He kissed her tenderly. 'Lord, I wish you weren't covered in bruises. I can't wait to make love to you.'

'What bruises?' asked Davina, kissing him back.

'Davina! We can't possibly . . .'

'What bruises?' And she slid down into the bed, pulling him down with her.

'I might hurt you. I don't . . .'

'What bruises?' she repeated for the third time, her hand on the button on his pyjamas.

'You're right,' Max agreed thickly. 'What bruises?'

Harlequin *Presents*

Coming Next Month

Available in November wherever paperback books are sold, or through Harlequin Reader Service:

In the U.S.
P.O. Box 1397
Buffalo, N.Y.
14240-1397

In Canada
P.O. Box 2800, Postal Station A
5170 Yonge Street
Willowdale, Ontario M2N 6J3

Could she find love as a mail-order bride?

MARIANNE WILLMAN
PIECES OF SKY

In the Arizona of 1873, Nora O'Shea is caught between life with a contemptuous, arrogant husband and her desperate love for Roger LeBeau, half-breed Comanche Indian scout and secret freedom fighter.

Available now at your favorite retail outlet, or order your copy by sending your name, address and zip or postal code along with a check or money order for $5.25 (includes 75¢ for postage and handling) payable to Worldwide Library Reader Service to:

In the U.S.	In Canada
Worldwide Library	Worldwide Library
901 Fuhrmann Blvd.	P.O. Box 2800, 5170 Yonge St.
Box 1325	Postal Station A
Buffalo, New York	Willowdale, Ontario
14269-1325	M2N 6J3

Please specify book title with your order.

SKY-H-1R

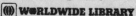 **WORLDWIDE LIBRARY**

Explore love with Harlequin in the Middle Ages, the Renaissance, in the Regency, the Victorian and other eras.

Relive within these books the endless ages of romance, set against authentic historical backgrounds. Two new historical love stories published each month.